Pine Forest Christmas

Up North Stories, Volume 1

Bonnie Oldre

Published by Bonnie Oldre, 2023.

This is a work of fiction. Similarities to real people, places, or events are entirely coincidental.

PINE FOREST CHRISTMAS

First edition. December 15, 2023.

Copyright © 2023 Bonnie Oldre.

ISBN: 979-8223335412

Written by Bonnie Oldre.

Chapter One

Emma Thompson, a tall, serious-looking thirty-year-old brunette, turned the house key in the front door and stepped out of the cold of an early November morning and into the entryway of her childhood home in Pine Forest, Minnesota. She paused, looked around, and asked herself, "What was I thinking?"

It was the first time she was back in the house, since helping Lily clean it out after their parent's funeral. With dismay, she noted that the living room wallpaper, which she remembered as cheerful, was stained, and peeling off the walls, where dampness had seeped into the plaster behind it during the years that the house was empty and unheated. Her parent's familiar furniture was still in place, but the house had a damp smell and a feeling of abandonment.

Well, it was too late for second thoughts, now. Six months ago, Harry had announced that he wanted a divorce to "find himself" only to find himself, within days, back home with his mother. Emma had decided that the past decade spent with Harry had been a big mistake, and she felt an urgent need to start over.

They didn't have children, so the divorce was quick and painless. She discovered that what she mostly felt about Harry leaving her was relief to be rid of him and his endless grousing. Nothing was ever good enough for him. According to him, his mother was a better cook. And, she didn't keep house like his mother. Never mind that his mother didn't have an outside job, but Emma did.

Harry and Emma had agreed to sell their house—their only major asset—and split the proceeds. That was when Emma began to think about moving back home. With her share of the profit, she could move into her parent's old house, take a year off from work, and finally write her novel.

The only family still in her hometown was her sister, Lily, who had married her childhood sweetheart, Frank, and their kids. And, a few cousins who still lived in the area. Most of her childhood friends had left town for school, or to find work, and had never returned. Emma, herself, had only been back for the occasional holiday visit with Lily and her family.

When Emma's parents had died in a car accident on icy winter roads, several years ago, she and Lily had inherited the family home. Lily had taken care of the house as best she could, but she didn't have much time or money to put into it.

Frank worked at the lumber mill, which paid well enough. But there weren't any jobs in town that paid enough for Lily to work, while also paying for childcare for their three kids, so they got by on Frank's income.

Lily had often suggested selling the family home. And Emma knew it was because she needed the money, but Emma had resisted the idea. She just wasn't ready to cut the tie to their childhood home, yet.

After Emma's divorce, when Lily mentioned the possibility of selling the house, again, Emma offered to buy out her sister's share and move home. That meant spending a big chunk of her nest egg, but it was only fair to Lily.

Lily had eagerly embraced the idea. She was thrilled that she would have her big sister living close by, again, and have some extra money. Lily had made sure that the electricity, water, and gas were turned on before Emma got there.

Now, as Emma walked through the rooms and noted the signs of a mouse invasion, the deteriorating carpeting and wallpaper, and the outdated appliances, she began to wonder how long the rest of her divorce settlement money would last.

Emma had deferred her dream of becoming a novelist while she was married. Harry had poo-pooed it as a pipe dream and insisted she do something practical. So, she had used her typing skills, honed while writing papers in college, to work in a series of offices, before settling back at her alma mater, in the office of the University of Minnesota's maintenance department. The job was deadly dull, but it had paid the bills. Harry occasionally worked, but mostly drank beer and watched TV. She was happy to give up that job along with Harry.

Emma was upstairs in her old bedroom, when a loud knocking on the front door, followed by laughter, voices, and footsteps, interrupted her train of thought.

"Hello, are you here?" Lily called out.

"I'm up here," Emma called back.

Her sister, Lily, came bounding upstairs, as full of energy as ever, her blond curls bouncing, and her blue eyes sparkling. She was trailed by her three kids: Jenny, age six, with red hair, Tommy, age four, with blond hair and freckles; and Cindy, age two, with dark curls, like her dad.

"Aunty Emma," shouted Tommy, the most outgoing of the three kids, "Are you going to live in Grandma and Grandpa's house?"

"Yes, I am." She beamed at him. All the other kids started dancing around, asking questions, and talking at once. Lily shooed them out of the room and Emma heard a thunder of little feet running down the stairs, followed by the plaintive cry of, "Wait for me." In Cindy's high-pitched baby voice. "Come on, then," Jenny called to her.

"Thanks for getting everything ready for me, sis," Emma said.

"No problem. There's butter, milk, and eggs in the fridge, and a loaf of bread, some peanut butter, and coffee in the cupboard. But tonight, I want you to come over for supper. Around six?"

"Thanks, Lily. That sounds lovely. Shall I bring something?"

"Just yourself. It's going to be just hotdish, I'm afraid. That's what the kids like."

"Sounds good. Is it a tater-tot hot dish?"

"Yup, that used to be our favorite. Do you still like it?"

"Love it," Emma said, wondering if she did. It had been years since she'd last had it.

"What do you think of the old place," Lily asked.

Emma grimaced. "It needs some TLC. I guess I expected it to be like it was when Mom and Dad lived here. But, of course, it isn't. It hasn't been lived in for years. Has it?"

"No. It's been about three years, now, since they passed away. Jenny kind of remembers her grandparents. I have pictures of them at home, so that helps. Tommy was too little, so he doesn't remember them, and Cindy wasn't even born, yet. But I always tell them, "That was Grandma and Grandpa's house" whenever we pass by. Sorry, I didn't do more with the place. I did what I could."

"Oh, I know. Don't worry about it. I could have come up more often, too. I'm sure I can get the place back in shape in no time. Maybe by Christmas time."

"In less than two months?" Lily looked skeptical. "Things take longer up here than you think. The local hardware store only stocks the basics. Most repair jobs require a trip to Grand Rapids, and that's a ninety-mile round trip."

"Yeah, I know. This is my hometown, too. Things probably haven't changed, too much."

"No, not too much. Maybe not as much as they should have," Lily said. "Are you bringing in your own furniture?"

"Eventually. It's in storage, for now. I figured I'd do some painting and maybe get some new carpeting, and so on before I totally move in. And, we have to figure out what to do with the furniture that's already here. You can take what you want, and maybe we'll sell, or give away the rest. I just brought what I could get into the car. I stuffed in a futon, which is lucky. The mattress on my old bed seems kind of damp and mildewy. Can you and the kids help me haul it out and haul my stuff in?"

"Of course. Let's go."

Within a couple of hours, the car was unloaded, the futon was on the bed, and the old mattress was sitting out by the trash. After a peanut butter sandwich lunch, Lily and the kids went home for afternoon naps, and Emma sat down with a second cup of coffee while contemplating where to install her office, which consisted of only a computer, a printer, and a box of printer paper.

She decided the little room between the kitchen and the living room, that her mother had used as a sewing room, would do. After setting everything up, she decided that tomorrow she would start writing her novel. But, right now, she also needed an afternoon nap and a shower, before heading over to Lily's house for supper.

There was a loud knock on the door. Emma opened it, thinking Lily had forgotten something, and was surprised to see a handsome stranger, a tall, dark-haired man, wearing jeans and a thick flannel shirt, on her doorstep.

"Hi, I'm Sam Mitchell," he said. "I live next door. Maybe your sister mentioned me?"

Emma thought for a second. "Oh, yes, Sam. She did mention you. You've been keeping the driveway plowed out in the winter, and cutting the grass in the summer, these past few years. Thanks for that."

Emma had imagined a much older man when Lily talked about him. Maybe a retired man, with time on his hands, not this strapping thirty-something-year-old, with such a nice smile.

"Come in, won't you? I was just about to have a cup of coffee; won't you join me?" she asked.

"Thanks, I don't want to get in the way. I just stopped by to introduce myself and to ask if you want to continue the arrangement."

"Oh, ahh...sure. Yeah, probably," Emma stammered. "I think so. I guess."

He laughed. "So, you're sure about that?"

She laughed, too. "You just caught me off guard. I'm not sure what the arrangement is. But, if my sister thought it was okay, I'm sure it is. Are you sure you can't come in for a cup of coffee?" Something about his smile made her want to continue their conversation. "By the way, my name is Emma Thompson."

She held out her hand and he shook it. His hand was firm and his grip confident.

"Okay, if you're sure I won't be in the way." He stepped inside and wiped his feet, carefully, on the doormat. He looked around. "The place hasn't changed much since your parents lived here."

"I suppose not," Emma said, hesitantly. "It seems a little neglected, but I hope to get it back in shape, eventually."

"Oh, so you're planning to stay for a while?"

"Me? Yeah. At least for the time being," Emma said. At least until the money runs out, she thought. "Let's go into the kitchen for that coffee."

Emma retrieved her cup from the end table next to the couch, led him into the kitchen, and poured each of them a cup of coffee. "I'm sorry, I don't have any sugar, but I do have milk. Would you like some?"

"No, black is fine for me," he said.

"Have you lived here in Pine Forest for long?" Emma asked. "You look kind of familiar. But I don't think I went to school with you."

"I've been here about five years, now. My folks used to have a cabin, down the road, he gestured east. So, you probably saw us around town. We were some of the summer people."

"Oh, yeah. I bet that's it." A picture of a handsome young teenage boy, with dark, wavy hair hanging over his eyes, sitting on a bench outside of the local grocery store, with a can of pop in his hand, came to her mind. "Do your parents still own the cabin?"

"No, they sold it, years ago," he said.

"So, what brought you back to Pine Forest?"

"Happy memories," a shadow crossed his face. "We always had such great times, up here. How about you? What brings you back?"

"The same, I guess. And, the house, of course. My sister and I inherited it when my parents died."

"I'm so sorry, about that. It was a tragic accident. They were such great people."

"Thanks. Yeah, they were. And it was a shock—the accident." She paused and stared into her coffee cup, then took a deep breath. "But life goes on. I'm sure they wouldn't want Lily and me to dwell on it."

"No, I'm sure not." Sam studied the back of his hand. "Do you have a job up here?"

"No, I'm, um…going to try to write." Emma was uncomfortable saying she was a writer until she had something published. Some of the advice she'd read advised against talking too much about the process.

"Really? That's great."

She studied his face, for a moment, trying to gauge his sincerity. "Yeah, I thought that the house should be lived in. And, I'd try to get started. I haven't written much, yet."

"Well, I wish you the best. It's great to have a goal, beyond just living and paying the bills." A shadow fell across his face, again. "Anyway, like I was saying, I take care of the snow removal and mowing. I used to invoice your sister twice a year in December and June. We can continue that arrangement. If that suits you."

"Sure, no problem, just send the bills to me. Or, drop them by."

Soon, the conversation turned to how soon it would snow, and then Sam declared he had to get going.

Emma saw him out and then sank onto the couch and closed her eyes, trying to get a short nap. But all she saw was the vision of Sam's face. *I shouldn't even notice him.* She scolded herself. *The last thing I need is the distraction of a relationship.*

The lamp on the side table flickered. She briefly opened her eyes and wondered, groggily, if it was just the light bulb or the electrical wires. As she recalled, her mother had said something about getting the house rewired, shortly before the accident. What would she do if she needed an electrician? Emma turned out the lamp and closed her eyes, again.

The sound of mice rustling around and squeaking startled her and she sat up, wide awake. What if they chewed through electrical wires? Would that short out her computer? She ran and unplugged it. First things, first, she decided, the nap would have to wait. She needed to make a trip to the hardware store for a surge protector and some mouse traps.

Chapter Two

The bell at the top of the door jingled as Emma entered the Pine Forest Hardware store. A woman who had been stocking shelves slowly approached the checkout counter and then smiled.

"Emma? Is that you? I heard that you moved back home," she said.

"Yeah, hi. It's Tania, right?" Emma said.

"Yup. So how have you been? Not so good, I guess. I heard your marriage hit the skids," Tania smiled again, showing off uneven and stained teeth.

"You heard right." Emma remembered that Tania had always been a little too blunt. "How have things been for you?"

"Can't complain. Every night is a party." She laughed a throaty laugh that spoke of cigarettes and whiskey. "Come down to the Big Bear Lodge, any night, and join the party. As I recall, you used to party with the best of us."

"Great, maybe I'll do that," Emma said. She wasn't anxious to rehash her misspent youth, so she'd stick with the reason she was there. "I was wondering, you don't happen to have a surge protector and some mouse traps, do you?"

"Let me see. I'm pretty sure we have mouse traps. Follow me." She led Emma to aisle number three and pointed. "Top shelf."

Just then a large black and white cat appeared and rubbed up against Tania's legs.

"Stupid cat." Tania shoved it aside with one foot. "You'd think it would have been run over in the parking lot, by now. But, no such luck." She laughed again. "Say, you wouldn't be in the market for a cat, would you?"

"You mean this one?" Emma leaned over and scratched it behind its ears. "What do you call it?

"Lucy. No, I can't give her away, she's the store's cat. Jerry would kill me. But this stupid thing is always having kittens. There are a half-dozen of them in a box at the back of the store."

"Really? Can I see them?" To Emma, kittens were about the cutest things around. But Harry had been allergic to cats, so she hadn't been able to have one.

Tania led her to a cardboard box with an old bath towel in it, and a bunch of sleeping kittens. Emma knelt next to the box and petted their little heads with one finger. "They're so little. How old are they?"

"A few weeks old."

"So, not ready to be separated from their mom, yet."

"Probably not yet, but soon. Interested?"

"Sure, I'll take a couple. I hear they do better in pairs."

Tania looked at her, skeptically. "Okay, if you say so. You can have the pick of the litter."

Emma looked them over, a couple of them were orange-striped. Two were black and white, like their mother. One was all black and one was grey and white striped.

"They're all so cute. I can't choose. Let the neighbor kids have their pick, and save the last two for me," Emma said.

"You got it," Tania said. "Still want the mouse traps?"

"Yeah, I better. It'll be a while before I get the kittens, and I'm not sure how much of a difference a couple of tiny kittens will make, anyway."

"You'd be surprised. Mice seem to avoid cats and will probably move on, once you have the kittens in the house. We don't have much of a problem, here, despite stocking grass seed, and other things mice like to eat."

"Sounds good," Emma said.

Tania rang up her purchase of mouse traps.

"What about a surge protector? Do you have those?"

Tania checked the computer. "I guess not. I can order some in. Or, they might have some at the Gas and Go. They stock some electronics."

"Okay, I'll check there. If not, I guess I'll order it from Amazon, or make a trip to Grand Rapids" Emma said. "Also, do you know anyone who does electrical work?"

Tania seemed annoyed that Emma wasn't willing to wait for her to order the surge protector. She plunked the mouse traps into a plastic bag and dropped it on the counter in front of Emma. "Nope. I don't know. You can check there." She gestured toward the bulletin board. Then she fished a pack of cigarettes out from under the counter, headed to the door, stepped outside, and lit a cigarette. Hugging her sweater, she sheltered against the cold wind.

Emma took her bag and scanned the overcrowded bulletin board. She found a tattered ad for Edge Electrical. "No job too big or too small," it said. She took a picture of the ad with her phone. She'd ask Lily and Frank, tonight, if they would recommend that company.

She was about to turn away when another ad caught her eye. It was for the Itasca Writers' Conference, scheduled for the week before Christmas, at a resort outside of International Falls. She stopped to look at it more closely. There would be classes, workshops, and chances to join critique groups and talk to editors and literary agents. One of the featured speakers was the renowned Minnesota writer, Brent Brugger. But, could she still get in? Maybe it was already fully booked. And, how much was it? Could she afford it? After the electrician, and who knows what else that might crop up? Well, it was something to consider. She took a picture of that, too. She'd have to look at their website and think about it.

Chapter Three

Gas and Go didn't have any surge protectors, either, so Emma undertook the nearly hour-long drive to the nearest large discount store and rolled her cart around loading up on groceries, cleaning products, cat supplies, and a variety of other items, as well as the surge protector. Then she stopped at the home goods store and got drop cloths and wallpaper removing supplies, and paint.

At the back of her mind, a little voice kept reminding herself that she should be writing, but she refused to listen. A day or two of adjustment was to be expected, after all. By the time she got home, there was only time to take a shower and get to her sister's house for dinner.

Her sister and brother-in-law endorsed her choice of electricians. Soon, the electricians were working on her house, tracking in mud, and then snow, as the month drew on. Days went by as they completed their work. Meanwhile, Emma moved her laptop from room to room, trying to stay out of their way. But the noise distracted her.

One day she took her laptop to the Moose Café, to try to get some work done. But, after a parade of former neighbors and classmates stopped by her booth to say hello and recite their life's story, she gave up and drove to Grand Rapids. There, she found her way to a bookstore, and killed a couple more hours, browsing for everything from home maintenance books, to books on how to write a novel, leaving with a heavy bag full of books.

After that, Emma gave up on trying to write while the electricians finished their work. Instead, she cleaned up after them, emptied mousetraps, and cleaned several years' worth of dirt and dust out of the house.

Once the electricians finished, she threw drop cloths over the living room furniture that she piled into the middle of the room, and began to scrape off wallpaper.

Then, the kittens moved in—the black one, a boy she named Midnight, and the grey and white striped one, a girl she named Tips. They solved the mouse problem. It seemed Tania had been right, and the mice moved out when the cats moved it. But they also provided an added distraction, playing around in the strips of damp wallpaper, and tracking it all over the house.

After scraping wallpaper until lunchtime, Emma sat down at her computer and tried to add words to her document, optimistically entitled Novel Number One. So far, other than transcribing a few handwritten notes that she'd brought with her when she moved in, the muse eluded her. She spent most of her 'writing time' reading one of the several books on how to write a novel that she'd picked up at the bookstore. That counted, too, she decided. At least she was working on writing.

Now, as she stared at the blinking cursor, she decided that drastic action was required. If the Itasca Writer's Conference wasn't sold out, she would attend it. The $2,000 was a big hit to her nest egg, but she had to do something to kick-start this novel. She looked it up and dialed the number. She was in luck, they told her. They'd had a cancellation and took her credit card information.

With that in place, she had something to put on her calendar. As she entered it on her phone, she noticed how empty the rest of the month was. Except for Thanksgiving dinner with her sister, she had nothing else planned. So why had she felt so busy? And, why had she gotten so little done on her novel?

I've been busy, but most of it was a mere distraction. A distraction from what? She asked herself. Obviously from writing. And why? Maybe Harry had been right, all along. Maybe she really wasn't a writer.

Emma slammed shut her laptop and strode through the living room, observing the walls nearly stripped clear of wallpaper.

At least this is something tangible. Something that I can do, she thought. She picked up her tools and climbed back up on the ladder, determined to finish it, no matter how long it took. After that, I'll head out to the Big Bear Lodge. I deserve to celebrate a job well done.

Chapter Four

Emma stepped into the semi-darkness of Big Bear Lodge. Everything looked and smelled familiar. The same smell of spilled beer. The same worn wooden floor. The same red vinyl seats on the swivel stools lining the bar, and many of the same people, who she'd shared drinks with on the rare occasions when she made the trip home over the past twelve years, perched on those stools.

"Hey, look who's here. It's Emma. The town's soon-to-be-famous author, Emma Thompson." Tania called out, from the shadows at the back of the bar, where several tables surrounded the pool table. "Come on back and join the party."

Emma raised a hand in greeting, and strolled in their direction, as she felt the heat rising in her cheeks. Who had been blabbing about her, she wondered. It must have been Sam. He was the only one, besides her sister, who knew about her plans. And Lily didn't hang out with any of these people. Just goes to show, she couldn't trust him to be discrete.

She stopped to order a beer and then carried it to join Tania and her friends. Tania introduced her to those she didn't already know.

"This is Jessie," Tania said, pointing to a girl in tight jeans, high heels, and suspiciously blond hair that didn't match her dark eyebrows.

"Hey, how's it going? So, you're an author?" Jessie said, with a smirk.

"Nope. Not yet. Just trying to write," Emma said.

"Trying, huh? What's the matter, didn't they teach you your ABCs in school?" Jessie said.

This evoked a chorus of laughter from the group.

Emma forced a smile. "Guess not. What do you do, Jessie?"

"I'm trying to be a forklift driver," Jessie said, which was followed by another chorus of laughter. "And, I'm succeeding at it. I work in a warehouse in Grand Rapids."

It looks like she's the ringleader of the group, Emma thought. She took her beer and sat with her back against the wall, and watched the pool game in progress. Neither of the guys playing was very good. There were more misses than pockets sunk, but it evoked a lot of trash talk and laughter.

The door opened and Sam walked in. Again, Tania called out a greeting and an invitation to "join the party." As Emma had done, he stopped at the bar for a beer and then strolled to the back of the bar.

"Mind if I join you?" He gestured to a chair at Emma's table.

"Not at all," Emma said, cooly.

She wasn't sure if she wanted to talk to him. He might repeat every word she said, once she was out of sight. On the other hand, why antagonize a neighbor? Especially one who was going to work for her?

"How's it going?" he asked.

"Not bad. I finished scraping the wallpaper off the walls in the living room, so I thought I'd celebrate by going out for a beer. And you?"

"I finished a job, and stopped by for a beer or two before heading home. Just my usual routine." Sam said.

Ah, a barfly, Emma thought.

Jessie came over to the table and stood a little too close to Sam. "How about a game?" she asked him. "Feeling lucky, tonight?" She laughed a throaty laugh.

"Okay," he shrugged. "Let me know when you're ready."

He turned back to Emma. "Need any help with the plastering and painting?"

Angling for another paid job, she thought.

"No thanks. There's no hurry to finish. I don't know when I'll get around to it," she said.

He looked at her as though puzzled by her coolness. "Okay. Yeah, I suppose you want to concentrate on your writing. Well, let me know. I've done a fair amount of painting in my day, and I'm fast."

"About that," Emma snapped. "I don't appreciate you talking about me behind my back."

"What?" He looked startled.

"Nothing. That is, never mind."

"No. I want to know what you mean about me talking about you behind your back."

"Some of these guys were teasing me about wanting to be a writer, and I thought—"

"Oh, I get it." He cut her off. "You thought I'd blabbed." He laughed. "Get over yourself. I didn't. But even if I did, so what? Is it supposed to be a secret? If it is, maybe don't sit in the café with your laptop."

Emma felt her face get hot, as she realized that she was the one who was responsible for the rumors. She crossed her arms across her chest. "Sorry. I guess I overreacted."

"Don't worry about it." He said, cooly. Then, he went over to the cue rack and started examining them.

Suddenly feeling very tired, Emma quickly finished her beer and headed for the door, while the rest of the gang was focused on the faceoff between Jessie and Sam.

Back home, Emma tried to ignore the ugly scars and gouges on the wall, left from scraping off the wallpaper. She switched on the table lamps and turned off the overhead light. There, now they were invisible. She sank into the couch and turned on the TV.

She felt a little lonely and out of sorts. She couldn't help but wonder what Jessie and Sam were going to do after they finished their pool game. What had Jessie meant when she asked him, "Did he feel lucky?"

Had she blown it with the hunky handyman? She asked herself. And, why should she even care? After all, she hadn't uprooted her whole life and moved this far north just because she enjoyed even longer and colder winters. She was here to write. And, write she would, but for tonight she couldn't do one more thing.

She laid down for a long-postponed nap. Soon, her two little kittens piled on top of her, and they all snoozed through the evening news.

Chapter Five

The next morning Emma was awakened by the sound of a snow plow. She was still on the couch. When she sat up, two little kittens tumbled off her, meowing protests in tiny kitten voices, and began running around and playing with each other.

She groggily stumbled to the window and looked out on a winter scene. Everything was covered by a soft, white blanket of snow under a brilliant blue sky. There was Sam, in his truck, snowplow attached to the front of it, plowing his way up and down her driveway. Obviously, he wasn't angry enough to ignore plowing her out. That was good.

She went into the kitchen, started the coffee pot, poured out some kitten kibbles for her little mousers, and then headed upstairs for a shower.

Today she would make a start on that novel, she thought, averting her eyes from the damaged living room walls. She had to have something, at least an idea, to take with her to the writer's conference.

She hadn't fully realized it when she'd said it last night, but she wasn't in any hurry to paint the living room walls. For one thing, she didn't have any idea how to plaster. From what she'd seen when her dad did it, it caused a lot of dust and didn't look that good when he finished it. She probably would need to hire someone to do it, and that meant another cash outlay. Besides, after weeks of disruption; first from moving, then the electricians, followed by the mess from scraping off the wallpaper, she was ready to leave well enough alone.

As she showered and ate breakfast, she remembered that her mother used to have a filing cabinet, which would make a nice addition to her office. She hadn't seen it in the basement. Had she gotten rid of it, or was it in the attic?

Emma ran upstairs, followed by little feline footsteps, and opened the door to the steep, spiral staircase leading to the attic. Midnight and Tips followed her up there, too, and started running and jumping around in the clutter.

Ah! There it is.

A tall four-drawer filing cabinet stood in the middle of the room, under a box full of old National Geographics. Emma sneezed, as she moved the dusty box onto the floor. She looked around at the accumulation of broken lamps and furniture, discarded clothes, and other debris. Too bad. Clearing out this mess was another chore that would just have to wait.

She tentatively tilted the cabinet, testing the weight. Yes, it was full. If she had any hope of moving it, even with help, it would first have to be emptied. She went downstairs and retrieved a few of her moving boxes that were still sitting in her bedroom, and brought them back up with her.

As she reentered the attic, a light sprinkling of snow drifted down on her. She looked up and saw daylight streaming in through tiny holes in the roof.

"Oh, crap! What next!" she exclaimed, and sank in a heap on the dusty floor. She covered her eyes with her hands and felt like crying. It had been one thing after another. Maybe this move-home thing was all one big mistake. After sitting there for a few minutes, the kittens came to visit her. She scooped them into her lap.

"We're not going to give up so easily, though, are we?" she asked them. They started to knead her legs, as though ready to settle in for a nap. They're little purrs and tiny needle-like claws digging into her legs snapped her out of her funk.

"I just have to face reality," she announced. "This is something that can't be put off."

She'd have to get the place reroofed. She looked up and examined the problem.

"I guess I'll have to get a job, after all, at least part-time, before the money runs out. I can't sit here with you all day. You'll have to find another place to nap. You'd better come with me."

She picked up the kittens, took them down the stairs, deposited them on the other side of the door, and then went back up to the attic.

She opened the top drawer of the filing cabinet. To her surprise, it was filled with shoe boxes. The top box was marked, ancestors. She lifted the lid and found it was filled with old black-and-white pictures. She looked at a few. There was Grandma and Grandpa Korhonen, Mom's parents. Other, older, photos were of people she didn't remember, but when she flipped them over, they were labeled with names and dates. She wanted to examine them more closely, but she decided that was for later. She didn't have time for it, now. She transferred the shoebox into one of the packing boxes. Another shoebox was marked "the kids." She started looking through it and then sat down on the floor with it and continued going through it. There were pictures from her childhood: school pictures, family vacations, birthdays, Christmases. Lost in nostalgia, hours passed as she slowly emptied the top drawer, browsing through the photographs, and reliving those happy times.

She glanced at her watch. Oh no, I've been up here for hours. It's nearly lunchtime.

"No lunch for you until you finish this," she announced, out loud.

She shifted gears and started shifting handfuls of files, full of old bills and correspondence, into the packing boxes. When she got to the bottom drawer, she paused when she saw a file marked "confidential." This one was too intriguing to ignore. She set it aside and emptied the rest of the drawer and then headed downstairs, taking the "confidential" file with her.

Emma took the file to the kitchen and started to pull out items. Inside she found passenger lists from a ship, copies of birth and death certificates, photographs, and a spiral-bound notebook. But why had her mother marked it confidential? She wondered.

Emma opened the notebook and blinked back unexpected tears at the sight of her mother's cursive handwriting, as she read "Chapter One. Start in the old country. Describe the conditions and what led to Grandma and Grandpa Korhonen to emigrate from Finland."

So, her mother was planning a book! From the looks of it, it was going to be a family history. But, why had she marked the file "confidential" and hidden it in the bottom drawer of the filing cabinet?

Emma called Lily.

"You've got to see what I found," she said when Lily answered.

"What is it?"

"It looks like something Mom was working on. Can you come over?"

"I'm just feeding the kids their lunch. We'll be there after that."

Soon, Lily and Emma were seated at the kitchen table, sipping coffee, and passing photos and documents back and forth. Meanwhile, the two little kids chased the kittens around the house, and Lily periodically reminded them "Be gentle. Don't hurt them."

"So, what do you think," Emma asked. "What was it all about? Did you know that Mom was gathering up this information?"

"No, I didn't." Lily paused. "Come to think of it, I happened to walk in on her, one day when she was writing in a notebook, and she quickly closed it. As I recall, I asked her what she was writing, but she didn't answer, she just changed the subject. I assumed it had something to do with work; that maybe she was writing something about one of her students. That's funny. I haven't thought of that in years."

"Do you think she was hiding it because she wanted it to be a surprise? It would have been like Mom to do something like that. She always tried to come up with Christmas gifts that were unusual and unexpected."

"Yeah, she was great. Wasn't she?" Lily's face softened, and she blinked back tears. She took a deep breath. "Or, maybe she was just shy about it. I remember her saying that she wished she was as bright and talented as her daughters. Maybe she just didn't want anyone to know about it, until it was done."

"What a Mom thing for her to say. I guess I'm kind of like that, too." Emma laughed. "I don't mean that I'm great. But, I kind of don't want anyone to know what I'm working on until it's done, in case I fail."

Emma explained what had happened yesterday at the bar.

"Oh, you won't fail," Lily said. "There's zero chance of that. You've always wanted to be a writer, and I have no doubt that's exactly what you will be."

"Thanks. I wish I had your confidence."

"How about this." Lily gestured at the contents of the box that were spread out on the table. "Why not finish Mom's project? I'm sure she'll be looking down on you, helping you every step of the way, if you do."

Emma looked skeptical. "I don't know. I have a project in mind. I kind of want to finish that, before I move on to something else."

"Well, that's one possibility. But you've been kind of stuck, haven't you? Why not set it aside, for now, and work on this?"

"I'll think about it." Emma started sorting through the documents and photos, making piles of similar items. "I suppose I could organize some sort of outline, based on this material. And it would be nice to finish Mom's work. I could add her name to mine when it's published. But who would be interested in it, besides you and me?"

"Well, my kids, of course, when they're older. And your kids, when you have some. And, if you expanded it into a family saga, maybe fictionalize it, a bit, I bet plenty of people would be interested. There are lots of those, aren't there."

"Yup, usually big, thick, multi-volume books. Enough to keep me writing for the rest of my life."

"Well, there you go. You have your life's work mapped out for you."

Lily and Emma both laughed.

"There are two other things before you go," Emma said. "First, can you take care of the kittens while I'm at a writer's conference?"

"When is that?"

"The week before Christmas."

"Sure, not a problem. Jenny will be out of school. I know that she and the younger kids would love to help me with that. What else?"

"I need a roofer. Who do you recommend?"

"First an electrician, now a roofer. Why?"

"I'll show you."

Emma led Lily up to the attic, followed by an entourage of kids and kittens, and pointed out the holes in the roof.

"Oh no," Lily said. "I had no idea. I never came up here. Luckily, you saw that when you did, before there was water damage. Why were you up here, anyway?"

"I came looking for that." Emma pointed to the filing cabinet. "I want to put it in my office. Can you help me get it downstairs?"

Lily looked at it, appraisingly, and then at the kids chasing the kittens around. "Okay, but first, let's get the kittens shut up in the bathroom and the kids out of the way, so we don't break our necks while we're at it."

A spirited kitten chase followed, and then the kids were ensconced on the couch in front of Sesame Street on the TV and warned to not move from that spot. Then, Lily and Emma slowly maneuvered the bulky filing cabinet down two flights of stairs and into Emma's office.

Once the kittens were released from their captivity, and the toilet paper they had shredded was cleaned up, Lily took the kids and went home. She promised to text Emma the name of a good roofer, once she talked to Frank about it. When peace was restored, Emma retrieved her mother's notebook and sank into the couch with it.

Okay, Mom, she thought. If you wanted me to find this, then you must help me decide what to do with it. With that, she started reading and making notes.

Chapter Six

Emma had been lost in visions of the past for hours, in the steerage of a ship, with her characters, who were making the choppy ocean voyage to the new world. When she finally looked up, it was dark outside, the sofa and coffee table were covered with notes, the kittens were sleeping next to her, and she was hungry.

A quick inspection of the fridge revealed there was nothing to eat except a few eggs, and that just didn't appeal to her. A burger and fries at the local coffee shop sounded better. So, she pulled on her winter boots, bundled up, and headed out. The Moose Café was only a few blocks, so she decided to walk, rather than drive. The fresh air would do her good.

Warm air, redolent of cooking odors, greeted her when she entered. There were only a few other people there. They glanced up, nodded, and then went back to their meals.

Emma slid across the cracked vinyl seat, into a booth against the back wall. A young waitress, maybe in her late teens, approached carrying a menu and a plastic glass of water.

"Hi there. Emma, isn't it?"

"Yeah, hi. Do I know you?"

"I'm Kim. You used to babysit for us."

"Oh, right! Little Kimmie. Well, all grown up, now. How are things? I see that you're working here."

"Yeah, my folks bought the place a few years back after the Olsons retired. And you? Where do you work?"

"Well, I'm not, right now. Just settling in. But I may be looking for a part-time job, soon, if you hear of one, let me know."

"Oh, right. I heard you had some work done on your old family place."

"You heard that? I guess news travels fast."

Kim laughed. "You know how it is in a small town, not much happens here. We kind of all wondered what would happen to the house after your folks died. I was so sorry about that. That was a bad year for ice on the roads."

"Yeah, it was. Anyway, I'm happy to see you, again." Emma picked up the menu and scanned it. "I was thinking of a burger and fries. Do you have that?"

"Sure thing," Kim pulled an order pad and pencil out of the pocket of the splattered black apron she wore over her jeans, and wrote down Emma's order.

Once alone, Emma breathed a small sigh of relief. Of course, she had known that she would constantly meet people she knew, here in Pine Forest. But it would take some getting used to. In the city, she could go for weeks, or longer, without running into anyone she knew, and socializing was mostly limited to nodding to her neighbors, or casual conversations with her coworkers. She realized she kind of missed the anonymity.

Emma took out her phone and started scrolling, as a way of avoiding further conversation. That worked until her food was delivered.

As she began eating, a large burly man entered the café. He seemed to be overly bundled up for the mild winter weather. He wore an oversized tan parka, with fur trim around the hood, a pair of heavy duck boots, and a fur-lined hat with ear flaps hanging down on each side of his seemingly enormous head.

Emma put down her burger and watched as he approached. He stopped at her booth, loomed over her, and removed his hat. His balding head was still enormous.

"Hello. Emma, correct? I'm Ray Morrow," he said in a low, rumbling voice.

"Yes, I'm Emma," she said, hesitantly.

He unzipped his jacket, retrieved a large navy-blue handkerchief from his belly pouch, and began cleaning the steam off his glasses. "I don't mean to intrude, but I wonder if I might join you. I was a friend of your mother's."

"Oh... Yes, of course... Please do," she stammered.

She scrunched her legs to the side as he slid in on the other side, bumping against her with his long legs.

Kim popped out of the kitchen and hurried to their booth. "Hi, Ray. The usual?"

"It's meatloaf tonight, correct?" he asked.

"Yes, it is. Extra gravy and peas?"

"Perfect! And, do you still have any of your mother's excellent apple pie?"

"Of course," Kim beamed.

"Save a piece for me."

With that settled, he turned back to Emma. "As a confirmed bachelor, I find it best to leave the cooking to others. I'm a regular, here. I suppose you're wondering who I am."

"Well, yes. I know most of the people in town. You must have moved here more recently."

"Yes, I moved here about five years ago, after I retired from the library faculty at the U of M in Bemidji. I met your mother, there. I used to get things for her, through interlibrary loans. She was starting a research project on her family ancestry. I suppose you know about that."

"No, that is yes. I didn't know about it until just today when I ran across some of her notes."

"How extraordinary!" he said.

"So, Mom was working on this for years. My sister, Lily, and I were wondering why she kept it a secret."

"I know your sister quite well. Such a lovely family" he said, and began eating with relish. "But, no, I don't know why your mom didn't want to talk about her project. After I moved here, we became reacquainted, and I would occasionally ask how the project was going. But she would just say, "slowly." I imagine she wanted to have something completed before she revealed it," he said. "Of course, that was not to be."

"No," Emma said, slowly. "Unless..."

"Are you considering completing it?" Ray asked, with a gleam in his eye.

"I don't know," Emma said. "As I said, I only just found out about it. And, if I did complete it, it wouldn't be a straightforward family history. I'm thinking more along the lines of working it into a family saga. Perhaps taking in more of the history and background of the Finish immigrant experience, as seen through the eyes of one family. It's just a thought."

"I see. I see." Now, Ray was positively beaming at her, as he steepled his fingers and scrutinized her face. "So, you're a novelist."

"Well, I wouldn't call myself that. Not yet."

"You're just like your mother, then." He chuckled.

"What?" Emma asked, startled.

"Not wanting to admit what you're doing until you have something to show for it."

"Oh." Emma paused to think, then laughed. "I suppose you're right about that. Plus, who needs the pushback from people telling you that you can't do it?"

"Who's telling you that?"

"Different people. An ex-husband, for one."

"Good thing he's an ex, in that case. Don't listen to the nay-sayers. Of course you can do it. Why not? Your mother was a talented, intelligent woman, and I'm sure you are, too. Anyway, you're not alone. There are other writers here, in Pine Forest."

"There are?"

"Yes, indeed. We have a writers' group that meets regularly. I am working on a science fiction trilogy. Others in our writer's group are working on other genres, such as mysteries and a memoir. We meet on the first and third Wednesday nights of the month, in Our Lady of the North church hall. We call ourselves the Wednesday Wordmasters."

"Wordmasters?" Emma laughed.

"Yes, there was quite a long discussion about the name. It took several meetings. My idea didn't make the final cut."

"What was your idea?"

"The Icy Scribes."

"Hmm, I wonder why they didn't go for it."

"Politics. It all comes down to who you know."

Emma laughed. "If I had been there, I would have voted for your idea."

"Yes, well, we'll never know if you're sincere about that. Anyway, you should join us."

"I don't know. I haven't written anything, yet."

"That's okay. We have a diverse group at all different levels. Some of us have been published, others are just beginning. You could just sit in on a meeting, and see if you're interested."

"I'll think about it."

"Good. I hope to see you there," Ray said.

Kim delivered his apple pie. "Are you sure you don't want a piece? He asked Emma."

"It looks delicious, but I'm full." Suddenly, she had a thought. "Hold on," she said to Kim. "Do you sell whole pies? I want to bring something to my sister's house for Thanksgiving."

"Yes, we can do that," Kim said. "But we'll be closed on Thanksgiving. Can you pick it up the day before?"

"That sounds perfect. Thanks! I'll just text Lily and see if she prefers apple or pumpkin, and let you know.

Lily texted back to get an apple. She was planning to bake a pumpkin pie.

"One thing ticked off my to-do list" Lily said with a grin.

"We don't usually have pie at our writers' group meeting, but we do have cookies and coffee."

Emma laughed. "I can see you won't give up until I agree. Okay, I'll give it a try."

Chapter Seven

Emma was standing in Lily's kitchen, slicing the pie, while Lily mashed the potatoes and the kids ran in and out of the room. Then, the doorbell rang.

"Are you expecting someone?" Emma asked.

"Oh, yeah. I forgot to tell you," Lily said. "Frank invited Sam. His family is scattered all over the place, and Frank doesn't want him to be alone on Thanksgiving. You don't mind, do you?"

"Me mind? No, not at all. Why should I? The more the merrier." Emma wondered why she felt flustered. And decided it was because she had been looking forward to family time.

Sam came into the kitchen carrying a couple of bottles of wine. "Hi, Lily. I found this Beaujolais in Grand Rapids. It's supposed to be pretty good this year."

"Thanks. You shouldn't have. Do you want to open a bottle?" She got a wine bottle opener out of a drawer and handed it to him. "There are glasses in that cupboard she pointed with the potato masher she was still holding."

"Hi Lily, he said, as he opened the bottle. "Nice to see you, again. Would you like a glass?"

"Sure, thanks," she said.

Frank poked his head into the kitchen. "Come on, Sam. The game's on."

"Frank, can you try to keep the kids out of the kitchen?" Lily called after him, as he disappeared, again."

"I'll try to corral them," Sam said. "Come on kids, let's help daddy watch football." As he led them out of the room. "I'll give you a piggyback ride if you promise to leave Mommy and Auntie Emma alone."

They all climbed on his back and hung off him, laughing, as he left, precariously balancing his glass of wine.

"You're spoiling them, Sam," Lily said, smiling.

Once Lily and Emma were alone, Lily said, "Maybe we'll have a few minutes of peace, now." Lily resumed mashing potatoes and stirring gravy. "What were we talking about?"

"How I met Ray Morrow at the diner."

"Oh, yeah. He's kind of a character, isn't he?"

"Yeah, and he was a friend of Mom's. Apparently, he was a librarian, before he retired, and had been helping her gather information on family history."

"Oh, yes, our Great-grandparents from Finland. Is it interesting?" Lily said.

"Very. I'm considering turning it into a family saga, as you suggested." Emma explained her idea.

After a flurry of activity, and the traditional complaints from Frank that he was missing the best part of the football game, everyone gathered around the table, and then passed around bowls and platters, filling their plates, while Frank and Lily also helped the kids.

"Shall we say what we're grateful for?" Lily asked the kids, once everyone was settled.

"That I get to sing Jingle Bells at school," Jenny volunteered.

"Aunt Emma's kittens," Tommy said.

"Pie!" said little Cindy, which made everyone laugh."

"Well, I am thankful for my family and friends, especially my big sister," Lily said.

Emma looked around the table. Everyone was smiling at her. "Right back at you, sis," she said. "And for my kittens, and Jingle Bells, and pie, too." She said, which elicited more laughter.

"Frank said, "For my lovely wife, of course, our kids, this wonderful meal, and that Sam could join us."

"What are you guys, the Waltons?" Sam said.

"Not usually, but we fake it during the holidays," Lily said.

"What about your family? What are they like?" Emma asked Sam. "Lily tells me they're pretty scattered."

Emma saw Lily's warning look, too late, and realized this was a sore subject.

"Um, yeah. My parents split up. My mom lives in Florida, but she's always off on some cruise. My dad lives with his girlfriend in California. My brother and sister live out of state, too, and are busy this year. So, here I am," Sam said. "Anyway, yeah, I'm grateful for friends, for this great food, and football."

To Emma's relief, the conversation then turned to how the Vikings were doing, and if the new quarterback was working out, and then to the weather.

"Speaking of weather, did Lily tell you I need a new roof," Emma asked Frank.

"She did. But it's too late in the year for roofing," Frank said.

"Why's that?" Emma asked.

"It has to be over 40 degrees for the sealant to work."

"But there are tiny holes in the roof, and snow is getting into the attic."

"Then, we need to cover the roof with tarps until spring."

"I can help you with that," Sam said to Frank. "No charge," he said to Emma.

"That would be great. Putting off that expense is another thing I'm grateful for."

Lily looked at Frank, who nodded, slightly. "Speaking of expenses," Lily said. "Frank and I thought that we should pay for half of the roof repair. It should have been done, years ago. And, if we'd sold it to anyone else, it would have been inspected and we'd have had to fix the roof before the sale, or reduce the price."

"No, that's okay," Emma said. "We settled on a fair price. I have a house without a mortgage; that's enough. Anyway, that money is for the kids."

They continued to argue over it for a bit and then agreed to discuss it later.

"Hey, there's a way to maybe win a little money," Lily said. "They're going to have a billiards contest down at the Big Bear Lodge. You used to be pretty good. Sam is entering it, I think."

"Yeah, I am. How about it, Emma? Do you think you might beat me? The top prize is $500."

"I don't know. Are you any good?" she asked Sam.

"Not bad. I figure I have a chance at winning, from what I've seen down at the lodge. Of course, I haven't seen you play, yet."

"When is this contest?"

"In a couple of weeks, December seventh through the ninth" Sam said.

"You should sign up. It'll be fun," Lily said.

"Maybe I will," Emma said.

Chapter Eight

The next day, Emma stopped at the hardware store to pick up a large bag of kitty litter and stopped to pet the store cat.

"Hey Emma," Tania said when she went to the checkout counter. "How are your kittens doing?"

"Good, really good. They're so much fun. And, you were right, I've had less trouble with mice since they moved in."

"Glad to hear it. By the way, have you heard about the pool championship?"

This, again? It was obviously the biggest thing happening, Emma thought.

"I have. Are you entering it?"

"Me? No! That would be a waste of an entry fee. I'd rather use that money for a pitcher of beer. But I heard you're pretty good, or that you used to be, anyway."

"Who'd you hear that from?"

"I don't know. I think it's common knowledge down at the lodge. Why? Are you, or aren't you?"

"I used to be okay."

"Yeah, that's what we figured. You know who's good? Sam Mitchell. He's entering. You probably couldn't beat him, anyway."

She's egging me on, for some reason. Maybe just for fun.

"Hard to say, I haven't seen him play."

"Well, he's usually down there on Saturday nights. Stop by tomorrow and see for yourself. Maybe even play a game or two."

"Okay, thanks," Emma said, noncommittally. "See you around."

Maybe it wouldn't be a bad idea to size up the competition before deciding to enter the contest. She'd see what she felt like, tomorrow.

Chapter Nine

The next evening, Emma looked up from her project. It was past five, and dark outside. Her lower back was stiff from sitting at the dining room table all afternoon. Midnight and Tips were snoozing in a pile in their basket in the corner.

She'd found she needed more space than she had on her little desk to sort out her mother's notes, so she'd moved her laptop into the dining room. But the chairs and the table height were far from ideal for hours spent reading, taking notes, and typing. She stood up and stretched backward. It would be nice to get out of the house and get some fresh air.

Some bar food and a beer at the Big Bear Lodge sounded good. And, she might get a chance to size up the competition and decide if she wanted to enter the pool tournament.

At the lodge, Emma took a booth where she thought she could watch the pool table, without being too obvious. Nobody was playing when she got there so after she ordered, she stuck a few quarters into the slots, pushed in the lever, and listened to the satisfying sound of the balls dropping and rolling to the end. Then she racked them up, broke, and started running the table.

It felt good, the cue stick, her stance, the stroke, the moment when the cue ball connected with the object ball, and especially when the ball dropped into the pocket. That was until she scratched. A familiar voice, behind her, said. "Bad luck!"

She turned slowly, and Sam was sitting on a stool against the wall, wearing an irritating grin. How long had he been there? She wondered.

"Yeah, well, can't win them all," she said.

"Playing alone?" he asked.

"I was," she said frostily. Then, turned her back to him, slowly chalked the tip of her cue stick, and continued to run the table.

"Want to play a game?" he asked when she finished.

"Maybe later. I think my food is ready. The table is all yours." She put her cue away and went back to her booth.

As she ate and sipped her beer, she watched Sam swiftly move around the table, sinking almost every shot. He was a fast player, maybe too fast. It seemed to Emma that he didn't take much time setting up his shots. Instead, he seemed to rely on his power, banging balls into the pockets, and his height, as he virtually lay on the table, balanced on one leg, to access the cue ball when it came to rest in the middle of the table.

One by one, the rest of the gang filtered in, and took up their positions around the pool table. Jessie and Tania showed up, last. They stopped at Emma's table, as she finished the last French fry.

"Hey, look who's here. It's Shakespeare.," Jessie said. "Written anything good, lately?"

"Maybe," Emma said. "And you?"

Tania laughed. "She's slumming. Hanging out with us plebs. Right?"

"If you say so," Emma said.

"Or, checking out the competition." Tania nodded toward Sam. "What do you think? I mean, about his game, not the obvious."

"Same answer for both questions. Not bad," Emma said.

Sam was splayed out, on the top rail of the table, one leg pointing in their direction. Tania and Jessie both burst into raucous laughter and left to join the rest of the crowd. Emma had to admit, it was not an unpleasant sight.

She continued to watch as he missed the shot. The object ball was frozen against the rail. He hit it too hard, and it missed the pocket. That was the second time that had happened. Was that his weakness? Emma ordered a second beer and sipped it, slowly, as Sam and Jessie played a game.

Jessie was pretty good. But Sam was better. He seemed to be missing shots, on purpose, just to make it a close game. But he made sure that he won. Then he racked his cue, got a beer from the bartender, and came over to Emma's booth.

"Mind if I join you?"

"Not at all."

He sat down across from her. "What do you think? Can you beat me?"

"Maybe. On a good day."

"Does that mean you'll play me?"

"Not until the tournament," she said. "Why give away all my secrets."

"I already know your secrets. I was watching, too. You're too cautious."

"Is that so. Well, you're not."

He sat, silent for a moment.

"Is that why you stayed married to a man you didn't love for so long?"

The question, which seemed to come from nowhere, startled her. "What do you mean?"

"You're not exactly heartbroken by your divorce. In fact, you seem perfectly fine with it. Even, happy."

Emma thought about it, for a moment, then looked into Sam's eyes. He was staring at her with a friendly, puzzled, expression.

"You know, you're right. At first, we were in love. Then, not. And, finally, I guess I was just glad when he ended it. I never would have." She raised her fingers to her mouth, as though to hold back the words that had just popped out.

They both turned and watched, silently, the pool game in progress. Jessie and Tania were playing.

"So, have you entered the contest, yet?" he asked.

"No, but I think I will."

"You should. What's the worst that could happen?"

"I could lose."

"Tell you what, if I beat you, I'll buy you dinner."

"What if we both lose."

"You've been watching the competition. What do you think? I think it's either you or me."

"And if I win?"

"You make me dinner at your place. Deal?" he held out his hand.

"It's a deal." Emma shook his hand.

Chapter Ten

For the next several days Emma went to the lodge, when it opened at eleven in the morning, practiced pool shots for an hour, had lunch there, and then returned home for an afternoon of writing. This gave her time to adjust to the table, try out the available cue sticks, and select her favorite, and avoid the competition, especially Sam.

On Friday morning, she anticipated following her new schedule. But when she crawled from under her comforter, disturbing the two little bundles of fur that had been sleeping on top of her, she found that it was unusually chilly in her bedroom.

True, the house was not well insulated and her room, on the north side of the house, was usually cool. But not like this. Had the temperature outside suddenly dropped? She stepped onto the floor; it was icy cold, ran over to the radiator, and felt it. It was also cold.

"Damn it!" she yelled.

The kittens looked at her, cocking their heads, and meowing. They knew their names, the words treat, numnums, and no. But this was a new word.

Emma shoved her feet into a pair of slippers, pulled on her fuzzy bathrobe, cinched it, and grabbed her phone. Then she paused. Who should she call? Her first instinct was to call Lily. But her sister was probably getting her oldest daughter, Jenny, off to school, and Frank off to work. With a sigh, she realized that she would have to call Sam. She decided to text him, instead. She didn't feel up to having a conversation with him first thing in the morning.

"Can you come over and take a look at my furnace?" she wrote. "The house is cold, and getting colder."

After sending the text, she carried her phone around, as she got ready for the day, anxiously awaiting a response. The first thing she did, when she got downstairs, was check the thermometer. It was already below 60 degrees. The temperature was normally set to 68 degrees at night. Checking the outdoor thermometer, she saw that it was just above zero. How long before the inside of the house was just as cold as it was outside, she wondered.

Finally, while sitting at the kitchen table with her hands wrapped around a mug of hot coffee, and the phone lying on the table next to her, it rang.

"Hi, Emma. What's going on?" Sam said.

"I think my furnace died. It's freezing in here, and getting colder by the minute."

"What's wrong with it?"

"I have no idea. It just doesn't work, that's all I know."

He laughed. "So, maybe it's just out of fuel."

"No, I had a delivery just the other day. That's not it."

"What kind of furnace is it?"

"Sorry, I don't know that, either. Can you come over and take a look at it?"

"I'm out on a job right now. I'll be there as soon as I can," he said.

While she waited, Emma put on an extra sweater, and then her winter parka, while sipping mugs of hot coffee. A couple of hours later, there was a knock on her door.

She flung open the door. "Finally! You're here!

"Yup. In the flesh." He grinned at her, stepped inside, and made a show of stomping the snow off his boots. "I told you I was out on a job. I couldn't just drop everything and come running."

"Yeah, okay. Anyway, come take a look at the furnace and see if you can fix it."

He trailed her down the basement steps, and over to her furnace. She watched as he fiddled around with it. Pulled a notepad and pen out of the pocket of his flannel shirt, made notes, and then knelt on the ground, unscrewed a hatch, and shone a flashlight inside.

"It's a bad igniter. These things go out all the time. If that's the only problem, I can fix it in no time. But I'll have to go into Grand Rapids for the part. I'll be back in a couple of hours and see if that does the trick."

"And if it doesn't?"

"If not, you might want to buy a portable electric heater from the hardware store or spend the weekend at your sister's house. Meanwhile, why not bake something? At least the kitchen will be warm."

Emma laughed. "And you'll have a treat when you get back. Right?"

"Hey, you are smart," he said. "See you soon."

Soon, as in a couple of hours, she thought. Obviously, she wasn't going to make it to the lodge to practice her pool shots today. Instead, she went to the grocery store for refrigerated cookie dough, and then home again to bake cookies.

Sam was right, soon the kitchen was cozy. She first shed her parka and then her sweater, as she baked panful after panful of chocolate chip and oatmeal cookies until every available surface in her kitchen was covered with cookies cooling on paper grocery bags.

When she ran out of dough, she left the oven on for warmth. She moved her laptop into the kitchen and had cookies and coffee for lunch while adding a few more pages of notes to the sprawling outline of her novel.

She paused. Was it time to take the plunge, and start turning the outline into the first pages of her novel?

When she'd signed up, she was told she should bring the first chapter or two of her work-in-progress to share with a critique group. That had seemed doable, at the time. But now she wasn't so sure. Creating an outline hadn't been easy, but at least she sort of knew what she was doing. But write chapters?

She got up and paced around. What if she wrote the wrong thing? What if she was laughed out of the room? What if it was boring? She wasn't sure she could face it. Should she drop out? But that would mean wasting $2,000 because the withdrawal date had passed. No, that wasn't going to happen. I'll write something, even if it's total garbage and ends up in the trash.

You're being ridiculous. If you can't write, it's better to find that out, now, and move on. Just do it, she scolded herself.

She opened a new document, saved it as The Korhonen Family Saga, a working title, spaced down, and typed, "Chapter One." Then, she sat and stared at the blinking cursor.

She'd read that the first page was the most important one. But, where should she start? Should she start with the family still in Finland, as her mother had planned to do? Or, on the ship sailing to America? Or at some later point, and then fill in the background with flashbacks.

As she sat staring at the blank page, a knock on the door interrupted her train of thought. With a sigh of relief, she closed the document and went to answer the door. It was Sam.

As he'd predicted, it was an easy fix. In about a half-hour the new igniter was installed, and Emma heard the welcome clanking of the radiators as the furnace turned on.

"All done," he said, as he reappeared from the basement.

"Thanks. You're a lifesaver. Can you stay for coffee and cookies?" she asked.

"Love to, but I can't. Other people are waiting. This cold spell is good for business. I'll take some to go, though."

"Okay, hang on." Emma found a container that she thought would work and started filling it.

He said, "I hear you've been practicing pool down at the lodge. How's that going?"

"Okay," she said. "How did you find out?"

He laughed. "I have my sources. Nothing stays secret for long around here."

"I guess that's true." She handed him the cookies. "Do you want a check, now, or are you going to send me a bill?'

He pulled a receipt out of his pocket and handed it to her. "Here's what the part cost. Just drop a check over for that amount."

She stared at him in open-mouthed astonishment. "Are you kidding? What about your time?"

"Don't worry about it."

"But I must pay you for your time. This is your job, after all."

"Okay. Whatever. Add on an extra $50 for my time."

"That's kind of low. Isn't it?"

"Call it the friends and family rate."

"Friends and family, huh? Doesn't that pretty much cover everyone in town?"

He laughed, again. "Not everyone. No."

"So, how do I rate?" she asked.

"Because I like you," he hesitated and then said. "I was wondering, do you want to hang out with me, sometime?"

"You mean, go on a date?" Emma was beginning to feel very uncomfortable about the direction this conversation was going.

"A date? No. Just hang out. We could play some pool together, for example. And maybe have a couple of beers."

"I get it. This is about watching me play, to discover my weakness."

"Isn't that what you were doing when you watched me?" he asked.

"No! I mean, I was already there when you came in. Was I supposed to run away? Anyway, didn't your spies already tell you all about my game?"

"My spies? Give me a break. No one told me anything, except that you'd been at the lodge every day, practicing. I just wanted to spend time with you, as friends."

"A friend?" Emma said, thinking that he seemed nice, and was handy, too. "Okay, I'd like that. But not at the pool table."

"How about cross-country skiing, then?"

"As in, outside, in the winter?"

He laughed. "Yeah. Is that a problem?"

"Well, to begin with, I don't have skis."

"That's okay. The state park has them for rent."

She paused to consider it. She hadn't been to the state park for years. She used to go there with her family when she was a kid, and they'd always had a good time. But that had been in the summer."

"I suppose I could give it a try. But I'll probably do more falling than skiing," she said.

"Then it's a date," he said.

Emma must have looked alarmed, because then he quickly added, "I mean, it's not a date. It's a thing that we'll do."

"Okay. We can do that, sometime. I suppose," she said.

"How about this Sunday? I usually take Sundays off."

"This weekend?"

"If that works for you."

Maybe an afternoon outside is just what I need to spark an idea. Emma thought. Or, maybe it's just another reason to procrastinate, a little voice at the back of her mind argued. That's okay. I have a couple more weeks before the conference. That's plenty of time, she thought.

"Sounds good. Text me on Sunday and let me know when you'll pick me up," she said.

As soon as he left, she regretted agreeing to go out with him. What a time suck. She was supposed to be writing, not jumping back into a relationship with all its complications. And, no matter what they called it, it was a date. At least that's what everyone in town would think. And what about Jessie? She was interested in Sam. And she wasn't the type to step aside gracefully. The more Emma thought about it, the madder she got.

Here I am, letting a man keep me from writing, again. Maybe Harry wasn't the problem, maybe it was me. Maybe I'm just not a writer, and subconsciously, I know it.

Her phone pinged with a text from Lily. "Don't forget, the kids are in the Christmas pageant at church on Sunday afternoon."

That's right, Emma thought. I can't go out with Sam on Sunday. I promised the kids that I'd go to the pageant.

She texted Lily back that, of course, she'd be there. And then texted Sam that they'd have to postpone their outing because she already made plans to go to the Christmas pageant.

She watched the cursor blink until Sam texted back a thumbs-up icon.

That was kind of rude, she thought. He couldn't even be bothered to type a word or two. Well, I don't care.

With that, she returned to the kitchen, opened her laptop, and sat staring at a blank screen. Then, her two kittens ran into the room, scampered around, attacking her ankles and each other, and then jumped up on the kitchen counters and started knocking cookies onto the floor.

"Down Midnight. Down Tips," Emma said, as she picked up the little fluff balls and set them on the floor.

They began batting around pieces of broken cookies, while she found plastic containers and packed up the rest of the cookies, and put most of them into her freezer. Her blank document was forgotten, for the moment.

After an afternoon spent typing a few words, and then erasing or changing them, Emma finally had the first few paragraphs written. She read it back and wrinkled her nose, highlighted it, and hovered a finger over the delete key.

No, she decided. Leave it be. At least it's a start. Ready for a change of scenery, she walked to the café for dinner.

Chapter Eleven

The welcoming odor of deep-fried foods and onions greeted Emma as she walked into the Moose Café. Ray was seated in his favorite booth and he waved her to come over and join him. His giant parka and fur-lined hat were on the bench next to him. He was eating a piece of blueberry pie.

"Come and join me," I'm just finishing up, but I'll have another cup of coffee if you don't mind the company."

"No, I don't mind at all."

Kim came over and took Emma's order—the fish fry.

"How's the writing project going?" Ray asked.

She grimaced. "Slowly."

"Ha!" he exclaimed. "You sound just like your mother."

"That's right," Emma laughed. "You told me that, didn't you? I wonder if she had the same problem I'm having. Figuring out where to start and how to organize the material."

"I'm not surprised. A family saga is a big project. Tell me what you've discovered, so far."

While she ate her dinner and Ray had a second, and then a third, cup of coffee, Emma explained the documents her mother had collected and the notes she had written.

"So, you see, there's so much material that I don't know where to begin." She concluded. "And, I want the first page to be so engaging that the reader will have to read on."

Ray chuckled. "That's a tall order. Here's a suggestion, just write scenes. Don't worry about chapters or pages. When you edit, you can rearrange to your heart's desire, and then rewrite the first page."

"Write the first page, last?" Emma laughed.

"Why not? By then, you'll have a better idea what your story is about."

"I don't know." Emma pushed her plate aside and rested her head on her fist. "I wanted to have the first 50 pages of my novel done before I go to the Itasca Writer's Conference, in case an editor or agent asks to see it. I'm sure everyone there will be a much better writer than I am. I'm afraid my manuscript might be bad. I mean, laughably bad. I just want the first few pages to be decent."

"I question your premise. First, that everyone attending the conference will be a better writer than you are. Unlikely. There will probably be a mix of skill levels. Anyway, what makes you think what you've written will be bad?"

"I don't know, it just doesn't feel like a story."

"I see. Well, you could bring your first few pages to the writer's group meeting and get a little feedback. You might get a better reception than you expect. Or, at least some suggestions for improvement."

"So, not necessarily a good reception," Emma said, hesitantly.

"One or two in our group can be a bit acerbic. It's nothing to fear. All part of the process. Another idea is making a visit to the Finland Minnesota Historical Society Heritage Site, which might spark some ideas. Have you been there?"

Emma sat up straight. "I forgot about that place. We went there on a field trip in grade school. As I recall, there are a lot of buildings depicting what life was like when the Finish settlers first got here."

"That's right. Unfortunately, I believe they are closed for the season, but I have some materials, which I've picked up on several visits, that I could share with you."

"That sounds great."

"In that case, I'll drop a package off at your house on my way to the café tomorrow."

Ray soon left, and then Emma finished her meal and walked home, humming a Christmas song on the way. This turned out to be a good day, after all, she thought.

Chapter Twelve

Emma drove up the driveway to the picturesque Our Lady of the North Church, with its white siding and blue roof, nestled in the snow against the star-studded sky, she noticed several other cars parked along the side of the church.

It had been a quick drive. Perhaps too quick. Although the church was located on the outskirts of town, it was only a five-minute drive from home. But then, almost everything in Pine Forest was within a five-minute drive. She wasn't sure she was ready for this, her first time at a writer's group meeting.

Over the past few days, she had resumed her pattern of practicing pool shots and lunch at the lodge, and then home for an afternoon of writing. She had followed Ray's advice, and written scenes as they occurred to her, without worrying about if they would be in that order after the final revision. She had spent hours reading about ocean voyages in the early 20th Century until she could envision herself as a passenger, so she started there.

She parked and took a deep breath, this was it. Nothing to be nervous about, she told herself. She checked, yes, the folded pages of her manuscript were in the side pocket of her purse.

She entered through the side door. A sign was taped to the wall, at the top of the staircase, "Wednesday Wordmasters" above a downward pointing arrow. She followed the sign, and the sound of voices and laughter, down the stairs to the church social hall. It looked mostly unchanged from when she attended church here, as a girl.

A small group of people, three women, and two men, stood next to the counter that separated the kitchen from the rest of the room, pouring coffee from a carafe, and selecting cookies from a tray.

"Emma," exclaimed Ray. "I'm so glad you could make it. Do you know everyone?"

"Mostly," she said. She knew the three women and Ray, but not the other man.

There was Sylvia, who used to work for the Post Office. She must be retired, now, because Emma hadn't seen her there, recently. Gloria, in her forties, worked part-time in the grocery store. And, Dottie, probably in her fifties, but trying to look younger, had been the church secretary. Maybe she still was and had arranged for the group to meet here. The person she didn't know was a man in his thirties, with long, dark hair that hung over one eye, which he kept smoothing back, and he wore a silk scarf around his neck.

"Everyone. Let's welcome Emma," Ray said. "She is writing a family saga, loosely based on the lives of her Finish ancestors. Be nice to her. We hope that she will join our group."

Ray introduced the members to Emma. "Sylvia is writing a memoir. Gloria writes romance. Dottie writes mysteries. As you know, I write science fiction. And, last, but certainly not least, Bryan writes literary fiction."

"Tries to write," Bryan said, with a small smile. "That's Bryan with a y, by the way."

"Indeed. Tries to write. That is so often true for all of us," Ray said. "Help yourself to refreshments, everyone, and then we'll get the meeting started."

Ray and the three other ladies headed to the nearest table. Emma poured some coffee. Bryan looked over the selection of cookies and reluctantly placed one on a napkin.

"I don't believe we're acquainted," Emma said. "You must be new to town."

"It's been a few years. I came up here to help establish the Arts Center."

"Oh yes, I noticed the wonderful new building next to the school. I'm sure it is a great asset for the town. I look forward to seeing what types of events are held there. Did you know that the space it was built on used to be a playground when I was in school?"

"Is that so? If you went to school here, you must be a local. But I don't recall seeing you around town."

"I just moved back home about a month ago."

Emma and Bryan took their coffee and cookies and joined the rest of the group. Ray seemed to be in charge. He asked the group how their writing was going. A few of them mentioned a word or page count. All of them talked about what had prevented them from writing, whether it was kids, grandkids, work, health issues, or holiday plans. Bryan said he was suffering from "writer's block" a condition that, as Emma knew, from her recent "how to write a novel" research, was often invoked by writers. She supposed that's what she had experienced, too.

When it was Emma's turn, she explained her recent move, and said, "I managed to get started. I have about ten pages written, thanks to some advice from Ray. He suggested that I write scenes without worrying about the overall structure of the novel. It helped."

He waved away her thanks. "I just passed along some advice I was given, years ago."

Emma said, "I have also had many interruptions to my writing: holidays, home repairs, frisky kittens—"

"Oh, I just love kittens," Gloria interrupted. "Did you take a couple of the kittens from the hardware store? They were so cute that I wanted to take one home, too. But my husband wouldn't hear of it. He says we have enough pets."

"Yes, I got the black one, and the gray and white striped one." Emma smiled. "Another distraction has been practicing my pool shots. I've entered the billiards competition at the lodge, which starts tomorrow."

This created a stir as the ladies asked her questions about it, while Bryan, with a pained expression, periodically poked at his cell phone.

"We should all go and watch," Gloria said. "And cheer you on."

"Oh, I don't know. The first couple of evenings are bound to be rather long and boring, especially tomorrow night, when we play sort of a round-robin, as they narrow the field to the first four people to win four games. The second night, we take turns playing each other, and the first ones to lose three games, is eliminated. The final competition, between the top two players, takes place on Saturday afternoon. That should be interesting. But, of course, I have no idea if I'll be one of the top two."

"From what I hear, while I'm at work, everyone seems to think it will be you and Sam in the finals," Gloria said. "I plan to come to the finals. Anyone else?"

Emma was getting used to how the gossip grapevine worked in Pine Forest, so she wasn't surprised that this barroom competition was the subject of conversation. But she was surprised by the assumption the winner would be either her or Sam. Surely, other people in the competition had some hope of winning.

"I can't. On Saturdays I have the grandkids," Sylvia said.

"Count me in," said Dottie.

"I don't know," Bryan said.

"I will try to make it," Ray said. But perhaps we should return to the subject, at hand," He glanced at the clock on the wall. "What we normally do, Emma, is go around the table, read from our current work-in-progress, and then the others have a chance to comment or ask questions. Who would like to begin?"

Gloria volunteered to read, first. Her work was full of adjectives and adverbs denoting longing and despair. Emma didn't usually read the romance genre, so she wasn't sure if this was to be expected. She remarked that the heroine seemed to be in some emotional distress. If that was the case, good job conveying that emotion. The other women mostly said "good work" and the like. Bryan said he never read romance novels, so he wouldn't comment. Ray pointed out a couple of places where there was repetition.

Others read from their pages, with similar feedback. The women were encouraging, with an occasional question that led to discussion about what they meant to convey, and notes made about possible revisions. Ray usually suggested small improvements. Bryan's comments were usually short and dismissive, as he declared he didn't read any of the genres presented. After hearing several such statements, Emma wondered why he had joined the group.

Finally, only Bryan and Emma were left. Bryan pulled a thick sheaf of paper out of his briefcase and began reading. Emma gathered, after ten or fifteen minutes, that his character, Max, was standing on a pier somewhere, in the fog, smoking a cigarette and contemplating his mortality. After the third or fourth metaphor about life, Emma drifted off.

She was brought back to the present when Ray said, "Are there any comments?"

The other women looked as confused as she felt, and only murmured, "Lovely. Amazing." While Bryan soaked in their praise. Ray mentioned that perhaps sticking to one, or at the most, two, analogies per paragraph might make the writing more approachable."

"I'm not going for approachable," Bryan said.

"Indeed? Well, anyone else? Emma, do you care to comment?"

"Well, no. Except, I haven't heard any of this before, I was just wondering..."

"Yes?" Bryan said, raking his hair out of his eyes.

"What is it about?" Emma said.

"What is what about?" Bryan said.

"The story. I gather that Max is standing on a pier, but nothing seems to happen. I was just wondering, what happened before this, or will happen after this? If that's not a spoiler."

Bryan pursed his lips. "Nothing happens. It's all internal. It's meant as a metaphor for the human condition. How we're all lost in a fog. It's not about something happening, it's about the use of language."

"Oh, I see," Emma said. Although she didn't see, at all.

Her hands started to sweat, and her throat began to feel scratchy as everyone turned to her. It was her turn.

"Emma, do you care to read? You don't have to, of course," Ray said.

"Oh, okay." She pulled her pages out of her purse with shaky hands and flattened them, noticing that the sweat made her hands stick to the top page as she did so. She stopped for a sip of coffee, and then she began to read.

Soon, Emma was swept up in her story. No longer fully aware of her surroundings, she was in an upper bunk, in the third-class passenger section of the ship, feeling her stomach roil as the ship pitched in the storm, smelling the stench of unwashed people crammed together for several days, and remembering the people and places she had left behind. And then, forgetting her discomfort while helping the mother in the bunk next to hers comfort her crying children.

When she looked up, all eyes were on her. Even Bryan. However, he quickly turned away and made a show of checking the time.

The women peppered her with questions about the character. Where had she come from? Why had she left? How did she get to the ship? How did she get the money for the trip? Emma made notes of their questions.

Ray just harrumphed a bit, and then said, "Good start. Nice touch, making your character sympathetic by having her help the mother with the small children. Perhaps a bit more dialogue and a bit less description?"

Bryan turned to her with a tight smile. "It's rather obvious. Isn't it? Poor girl, on her own, making it in the new world. Hasn't it all been done, before?"

Emma thought she'd like to reach over and twist his nose. Instead, she just said, "No doubt it has been done before. Probably, most stories can be boiled down to something that's been done before. Isn't your hero, standing in the fog, uncertain about what to do next, somewhat like Hamlet?"

Bryan stared at her, open-mouthed, momentarily wordless.

"Time to wrap things up," Ray said. "We'll see everyone in two weeks,"

"Except me," Emma said. "I'll be at the writers' conference."

"Oh, that's right. Thanks for the reminder," Ray said. "I will be eager to hear how it goes."

Bryan left quickly. The rest of the group stayed to clean up. Ray and Emma were the last to leave.

"I hope I didn't offend Bryan," Emma said to Ray, as he switched off the light before leaving.

"I'm sure he'll get over it. I think he's used to being praised, not questioned."

"I guess I'm just not familiar with that style of writing," Emma said.

"Who knows? It might be a best seller one day. Perhaps it will be a bit like *Catcher in the Rye*, in lacking a strong plot. Meanwhile, we all have our illusions."

Ray locked the side door and, with a wave, headed toward his car.

Chapter Thirteen

Thursday night was every bit as exhausting as Emma expected. After hours of play, she, Sam, and a couple of the barroom regulars, Tom and Jessie, had won four games each. Jessie was a good player, although not consistent. Her level of play declined as the number of beers she drank increased.

But Jessie and Tom had a cadre of supporters cheering them on, which must have pleased the bar owner. Emma knew that the contest entry fees didn't cover the prize money. But the contest greatly increased the size of the Thursday night crowd, and the amount of beer sold.

Emma went home, afterwards, dead tired, and fell into bed. The next day she slept in, until her two little kittens, eager for their breakfast, started jumping on her and attacking her feet under the covers.

"Okay, okay. I get the message," she said.

She stumbled downstairs, poured out their food, and started the coffee. Then she went back upstairs for a long, hot soak in the tub. By the time she was ready for the day, it was nearly lunchtime. Well, it would have to be brunch, today. She fried eggs and made toast.

After brunch, she sat down in front of her laptop and tried to get back into her story. But her mind kept drifting to visions of pool balls on a green-felt surface. She mentally reviewed the shots she'd missed. Some, she'd hit a little too hard, others too softly. Other times, she'd put too much, or too little, spin on the cue ball.

She also mentally reviewed Sam's shots. She had studied him, as he played, looking for a weakness. She was sure he had done the same to her.

Emma tried, repeatedly, to refocus on writing, but accomplished little. Finally, she gave up, closed her laptop, and decided to take the weekend off.

I'll get back to work after the tournament, she thought.

She took a book and cup of coffee into the living room, settled on the couch, and soon fell asleep. Her phone pinged with a text message, waking her up. Emma smiled as she read the message from Gloria. It was festooned with emojis of hearts, clapping hands, and confetti, congratulating her on making it to the second round in the pool tournament and wishing her good luck, tonight.

The second round proceeded much like the previous night. Except, it was an elimination. They took turns playing each other, and the first ones to lose three games would be eliminated.

Jessie wore even tighter jeans, higher heels, and a lower-cut top. An obvious tactic to distract her male opponents. It worked on Tim, who lost three games in a row and was eliminated. But it seemed to not affect Sam.

Why *should* it affect him, Emma thought. I'm sure he's seen her in even more revealing outfits, not to speak of completely naked.

Now with only three competitors left, the real competition began.

Sam won the next game against Jessie. But Emma played the next game against Jessie and lost with a scratch. As Jessie smirked at her, Emma berated herself for her poor play.

I can't let her get to me, she thought and resolved to concentrate.

The next matchup was between Emma and Sam. He broke and was running the table. Sam glanced in her direction before shooting at the 8-ball.

Was that a smug expression? She asked herself. Emma felt the anger building inside of her, as she battled for self-control. Is that it? After all my work? Am I going to be knocked out of the competition?

Sam hit the 8-ball too hard. It bounced back and forth against the cushions on either side of the pocket, and stopped, hanging on the edge of the pocket. He straightened up, and shook his head slightly, as though in disbelief. Then, hunched his shoulders, stalked over to his chair, and sat down.

Emma stepped up to take her turn. She took several deep breaths to calm her racing heart, and walked around the table, focusing on the plays she could make. Then, she played a slow and careful game. Nothing would be rushed. She examined each angle before making a shot, while trying to control where the cue ball would stop for the next shot. She avoided the blocked pocket, as she pocketed all her balls, and then tapped in. She looked up and smiled at Sam. He avoided looking at her.

Now, the tournament was even. Sam, Emma, and Jessie each had two wins and one loss. The next person to lose two games would be out.

Emma, buoyed by her win against Sam, played a slow and deliberate game against Jessie, and won. In the next game, Emma broke and ran the table, winning the game against Sam. In the final game, Sam easily beat Jessie.

Jessie was out, and Sam and Emma would move on to the finals.

Emma went home and fell into bed.

It's been fun, but I'll be glad when tomorrow is over, she thought, as she drifted off to sleep.

The next morning didn't get off to a great start. She got up late, again. As she tried to get dressed, her phone kept pinging with texts wishing her good luck. One from her sister said that Frank's parents were watching the kids, so they were coming.

Emma discovered that the shirt she wanted to wear had a stain on it, and she spent some time trying on different shirts until she found one that she liked. By that time, her hair was standing on end from static cling. After failed attempts to flatten it, she just pulled it back into a ponytail. Her black slacks became a cat fur magnet, and she couldn't find a lint brush. She improvised and got most of it off with scotch tape wrapped around her hand. And, the coffee pot wouldn't work. She finally rushed out of the house, feeling frazzled, without any coffee.

She got to the Big Bear Lodge a few minutes before noon when the contest was scheduled to begin. The parking lot was nearly full. She rushed in, out of breath, to see a crowd of people looking at her. Her sister and brother-in-law waved to her, and she spotted the Wordmasters in a booth, already sharing a pitcher of beer.

She rushed over to the pool table area, dumped her winter jacket on a stool, and then listened as the referee, the bar owner's son, explained the bar's rules. Including, that the first to win three games would win the tournament, and they would take turns breaking. He would flip a coin to determine who broke first. The coin toss went to Emma.

Emma went to the rack to choose her cue stick. But her favorite one wasn't there. She looked at them all, again. No, it was not there. Had Sam taken her cue stick? She looked closely at his. No, he didn't have it.

The ref came over to talk to her. "Are you ready to begin?"

"There's a cue stick missing. I can't find the one I've been practicing with," she said.

"I'll ask the waitress to look around the bar, but you'll have to pick another one, for now," he said.

Emma reluctantly chose her second-favorite cue stick, took it back to the pool table, and started chalking the tip, while the ref racked the balls.

Where was her favorite cue stick? It had always been there when she practiced. Had someone misplaced it on purpose? Was it Sam? But he wouldn't pull a dirty trick like that, would he? She wondered as a thumping in her head started.

She glanced at him, and he smiled back at her.

Was that a genuine smile, or a gotcha smile? she thought. Never mind him. Concentrate on the game,

She tested the weight of the cue stick, and slid it back and forth, preparing to break. No, her stance was off. She stopped, adjusted her stance, and went through the preparatory motions, again, and then broke.

It wasn't a good break, a few balls spread out and bounced off the cushions, but several stayed clumped around the 8-ball. Most of them were solids.

Emma stalked back to her chair and slumped down.

It was an open table and Sam's turn. He, of course, chose stripes. He pocketed a few balls but then missed when he tried to pick off a ball that was in the clump. At least he had loosened up the cluster of balls.

She had another chance! Emma picked off the solids, one by one, until only the 8-ball was left. She examined the angles, called the pocket, and made several preparatory strokes, stopping, each time, within a fraction of an inch of the cue ball. Then, she struck the cue ball.

The 8-ball rolled toward the corner pocket, narrowly missing a striped ball in its path, and fell into the pocket. And then the cue ball rolled in after it. Emma stood, frozen in disbelief for a moment, and stared at it in disgust. A scratch! She had lost.

Sam had the next break. He did so with an authoritative crack and the balls spread out all over the table. Both a solid and a stripe rolled into a pocket. He still had an open table and could pick either solids or stripes. He could hardly have been in a better position to run the table, and he did.

While he was doing that, Emma watched as the waitress searched for the missing cue stick, found it behind the coat rack, and returned it to the cue rack.

Behind the coatrack! How on Earth did it wind up there? Did someone hide it there? Wouldn't it have been found at closing time, if someone left it there, by accident, last night? She fumed. Pull yourself together. She scolded herself. One more loss, and you're handing Sam the tournament win.

While the ref racked up the balls, Emma exchanged cue sticks. She carried it back to the pool table and chalked the tip while enjoying its familiar feel. She blocked out everything and concentrated on nothing but the shots she was making, and planning for the next shot. She won the third game.

It was the fourth game, and it was Sam's turn to break. He blasted the balls, again. But luck didn't favor him, this time. The balls ricocheted around the table, bouncing off each other and the cushions, but none of them fell into a pocket.

It was an open table and Emma's turn. She examined the table, closely, chose solids, and ran the table. Now, they were tied, at two games each. The fifth game would determine the winner of the tournament.

Emma broke and a striped ball fell into the pocket. She examined her options. She saw a couple of easy shots. But then what? She might be able to double-bank a shot, into the side pocket. But if she missed, which was certainly possible, where would that leave Sam?

She looked some more, thinking about defensive positions, and saw a shot she could attempt that would leave the cue ball frozen to the cushion if she missed. She knew this was a weak shot for Sam. She followed that plan, and sat down, feeling confident that he would miss the shot, and she would have another chance to win.

Sam got up and paced around the table, examining every angle, then leaned way forward on the side rail, keeping one foot on the floor, made a bridge with his hand, brought the tip of the cue stick down, ever so gently, and the object ball rolled and fell into the pocket.

So, he could play carefully, when he needed to! Emma thought as she tensed up.

She watched, with mounting frustration, as he knocked one ball, and then another, and another, into the pockets, and finally pocketed the 8-ball, winning the competition.

Emma blinked back tears of frustration, as she walked past the crowd of people who had gathered around Sam to congratulate him and put away her cue stick. Then she walked over to Lily and Frank and joined them.

"Bad luck!" Lily said. "You nearly had him."

"You can't win them all." Emma shrugged, with attempted nonchalance.

"What was going on with the cue sticks?" Frank asked.

"Oh, that. I have a favorite, and it went missing. The waitress found it behind the coat rack. Weird, huh?"

"That is weird," Lily said. "If you had it, maybe you would have won another game."

"We'll never know," Emma said. "Speaking of the waitress, I wonder if I could get a cup of coffee. My coffee maker went on the fritz, and I haven't had one, yet."

Frank flagged her down, and Emma ordered coffee.

"I'm sorry about the mix-up over the cue sticks," the waitress said. "I don't know how that happened."

"That's okay. It's not your fault, I suppose someone left it there, last night." Emma said.

"I doubt it. I didn't see it there when I hung up my jacket when I got to work this morning," she said. "Of course, I might have missed it."

She went off to get the coffee, and the Wordmasters came to congratulate Emma for great games, saying how much they'd enjoyed it. Except Bryan, who trailed behind the group, mumbled an excuse about having to go, and quickly left.

Then Sam came over to their table.

Frank and Lily congratulated him on his win.

"Thanks. And thanks for the great competition, Emma." Sam said.

"Sure. No problem. And congrats on winning." Emma said, forcing a polite smile.

"The bar owner wants a picture of us, over by the pool table. If you can stand it."

"Why not?" she said and walked with Sam toward the pool table.

"I guess I owe you a dinner," he said.

"You do? Why's that?" she asked.

"Our bet, remember? If I won, I would buy you dinner."

"Oh, that. Don't worry about it," she said, thinking that she'd rather have a root canal than go out to dinner with him.

"No, really, I'd like to," he said.

"Sorry," she said. "I'm going to be super busy for the next few weeks. I need to get ready for a writer's conference, and then go to it."

"Oh, okay. Well, I'll check in after that," he said, looking puzzled. "You're not mad at me for winning, are you?"

"Of course not," she lied.

"You still get $200 for second prize, you know," he said.

"I know."

Emma forced herself to smile through the picture taking, and while accepting the second prize check and the smaller trophy. When she got home, she chucked the trophy into the back of the coat closet and sat down and cried.

Chapter Fourteen

After a good cry, a short nap, and a soak in the tub, Emma's thoughts turned to the future. And the immediate future was one without coffee unless she got a new coffee maker. With that in mind, she dressed and headed to the hardware store.

The jingle of the bell as she entered the store brought Tania to the checkout counter.

"Hi, Emma. How are you doing?" Tania asked.

"Okay, and you?" Emma said.

"Better than you, I bet. Tough break on losing the tournament."

"Yeah, well, you win some, you lose some," Emma said.

"Sure. But I heard there was a mix-up with the cue sticks. I suppose that didn't help." Tania stared at her with a taunting grin.

Emma felt a ball of anger rising from her core and took a deep breath. She wasn't going to let Tania goad her into saying something she would regret.

"No, it didn't help. I guess it got misplaced." Emma said. "My fault for not getting there, sooner, so I had a chance to hunt it down."

"Misplaced," Tania snorted derisively. "Yeah, that's what happened."

"What are you implying?"

"Nothing," Tania smiled, slyly. "Anyway, is there something I could help you find?"

"I need a new coffee maker. Do you have any?"

"I think so." Tania directed her to the back, where they kept the housewares. Emma found one and brought it back to the counter.

As Tania rang up the sale, Emma asked, as casually as she could manage. "Did someone say something about hiding the cue stick?"

Tania paused, then slipped the coffee maker into a plastic bag, and handed it to Emma. "No, nobody said anything. But there are a few people around here who like Sam more than they like you if you know what I mean."

"Do you have someone specific in mind?" Emma asked.

"No, I don't. I'm just saying that Sam has a lot of friends around here. While you took off after high school, and have hardly bothered to come back, since, and then suddenly show up, again."

"And, one of his friends might have wanted him to win, and wanted me to lose? Is that right?"

"Exactly. Anyway, why shouldn't Sam win? He plays all the time. Do you? I know you've practiced a lot, these past few days, but what about before that? Did you play a lot?"

"No, I guess not." Emma felt conflicted. She wanted to be mad at Tania. But what she said made a lot of sense. "I guess that's something to think about. See you later."

Back home, Emma unpacked her new coffeemaker and brewed a pot. While she waited for it to finish, she texted her sister. "I need to talk. Can you come over for a cup of coffee?"

A short time later, Lily was sitting with Emma at the kitchen table, drinking coffee and munching on one of the cookies that Emma had pulled out of the freezer, and zapped in the microwave.

"Are you feeling better?" Lily asked. "You seemed pretty upset when you left the lodge."

"Did I? I was trying not to show it. But I guess you know me too well. I don't like to lose."

"Yeah, I know. I seem to recall dodging some checkers thrown at me when you lost a game." She chuckled.

Emma smiled. "I guess I was kind of a sore loser, as a kid, wasn't I? But I've gotten over it."

"If you say so."

"Anyway, it's not just that I lost, but the way I lost. That hidden cue stick really burns me up. Who do suppose did that?"

"Are you sure it was hidden, and not just misplaced?"

"Well, you heard what the waitress said. It wasn't there when she came to work this morning."

"She said she didn't *think* it was there. She might not have noticed it."

"True. But then there was what Tania said." Emma repeated the conversation.

"Well, that does sound suspicious," Lily said. "It sounds like she's implying that it was Jessie."

"That's what I thought, too."

"Of course, she could just be trying to throw a little shade on Jessie. I have a feeling that Tania kind of likes Sam, too."

"Really? So, you think that both Jessie and Tania are after Sam?"

"Could be. After all, he's an eligible bachelor. How many other good-looking, young, single guys are around?"

"I suppose you are right. Most of the guys are old guys, like Ray, or married, or oddballs who live in trailers out in the woods, who rarely bathe and can barely speak to a woman."

Lily laughed. "You got it. And then there's Sam. Naturally, the single ladies are going gaga. But he only has eyes for you."

"Me? What do you mean?"

"Come on. You must have noticed how he's always looking at you, and smiling at you. I know he's been trying to get you to go out with him."

"I'm not interested in starting a new relationship, just now. Anyway, I figured that was just the way he was around women."

"Nope, just you."

Emma felt her cheeks grow warm, as she stared into her coffee cup, then she looked up at Lily.

"Do you know him, well?"

"I think so. He and Frank are best buds. They hang out together, doing guy stuff—fishing, watching sports, and so on. We've known him for years. Why do you ask?

"I hate to even think this, but what if Sam hid the cue stick?"

"Sam? No way. Why would he?"

"To win. He tries to play it cool, but I think he's just as competitive as I am. I watched him play pool with Tania. He eased off, to keep the game competitive, but he made sure he won, in the end."

"Sure, he likes to win. Who doesn't? But, no, Sam would never do something so underhanded. He won't even exaggerate the size of the fish that he's caught. He's like Dudley Do-Right."

Emma laughed at the comparison, suddenly feeling a weight lift, but then she started to feel guilty. I was kind of mean to Sam, she thought. I should try to talk to him.

The conversation turned to the upcoming holidays.

"Come to ten o'clock mass with us, tomorrow morning," Lily said. "Sam might be there. Maybe you can talk to him and clear this whole thing up."

"I'll try to make it," Emma said, feeling more festive than she had in a long time.

Chapter Fifteen

When Emma walked into the church, with Lily and her family the next day, she noticed Sam, sitting near the back. She nodded to him as they walked past, but he was at the other end of the pew, so she didn't get a chance to speak to him. Maybe she could catch him, later.

After mass, when Lily, Frank, and their kids went downstairs for donuts, Emma said, "I'll catch up with you." Then she hurried to catch up with Sam.

Outside, she called out, "Sam! Wait."

He turned and waited for her to catch up. "What's up?"

Emma suddenly noticed the gold flecks in his brown eyes, as he looked down at her, and it made her lose her train of thought. "I... I just wanted to congratulate you, again, on winning the competition."

"Thanks, but there's no need," he said.

"No, but..." She hesitated, as Sam continued to smile at her, waiting for her to continue. "I was kind of a poor sport. So, I just, sort of, wanted to apologize."

"You a bad sport? No." He laughed. "Well, I just, sort of, accept your apology."

Emma felt her face grow hot and was starting to regret this conversation. "I was kind of rattled because I got there late, and my favorite cue stick was missing." She started to feel more and more ridiculous, as she tried to explain.

"What do you mean, missing?" he asked.

"Didn't you know? It was behind the coat rack. The waitress found it."

"Is that what that was all about? I noticed you took some time choosing a cue stick, and then switched it later, but I didn't know why. How did it get misplaced?" he said.

She stared at him. If he was faking ignorance, he was a great actor. "Nobody seems to know. Anyway, that was no excuse for being so rude to you."

His face clouded over with anger. "Wait a second. You suspected me. Didn't you? That's why you were so mad."

"No, I... That is, I didn't know—"

He cut her off. "Just so you know, I had nothing to do with it. Now, if you'll excuse me."

Sam turned and stalked off.

With a sinking feeling, Emma stood, watching him leave. She wanted to call out after him, but she didn't think it would do any good. She turned and headed back inside. Good going, Emma, she thought. Now you've made it worse.

She got some coffee and a donut and joined Lily and her family. After a while, the kids ran off to play, and Frank wandered off to get more coffee and then stopped to chat with some of his pals.

Lily asked, "Did you talk to Sam?"

"I tried to, but he just got mad."

"Really? Why?"

"He totally didn't know anything about the missing cue stick," Emma said.

"Yeah, men can be clueless. But, why should that make him mad?"

"When I told him about it, he jumped to the conclusion that I thought that he had hidden it."

"Well, to be fair, you kind of did think that. What did he say?"

"He just said he had nothing to do with it and left in a huff. What do you think I should do?"

"Nothing, yet. Just let him cool off. He had kind of a bad experience with his last girlfriend. She was the suspicious and jealous type. So, he's kind of touchy about stuff like that."

"Really? Who was she? Anyone I know?"

"I doubt it. She wasn't from around here. A Rebecca somebody. I only met her a few times and didn't like her. She was kind of standoffish. Shh. Here comes Frank. We'll talk more, later."

Frank returned to the table. "What are you girls gossiping about?" he asked.

"Christmas," Lily said. "We were talking about where we should get together for Christmas. Weren't we, Emma?"

"Uh-huh," Emma said, playing along. "Of course, my house is kind of under construction."

"But it's bigger than our house. We don't care about the bare walls in the living room. Do we, Frank?"

"What? No." He shrugged, as though he was barely following the conversation.

"Remember how Mom and Dad always had a big tree in the living room, and stacks of presents under the tree?" Lily asked Emma. "I suppose the ornaments are still up in the attic, where they always kept them."

"Yeah, I think I saw them up there. But I don't have time to put up a tree and decorate it, this week. I need to get ready for the writer's conference. And, once I get back, it will be too late. All the Christmas trees will be sold."

"That's true. Well, maybe next year. Meanwhile, you can come to our house for Christmas."

Chapter Sixteen

The hour-and-a-half drive from Pine Forest to International Falls passed quickly. It hadn't snowed in days, so the roads were in good shape. When Emma arrived at the resort, she found an imposing two-story log and stone building, surrounded by snow-laden pines.

Emma parked and unloaded her suitcase from the trunk while wondering who else would be here, and how the week would go. She felt a little nervous about it. She had never been to a writer's conference before, and she wondered if she would stick out as a complete newbie.

She started to feel more at ease when she stepped inside. There was a cheerful fire burning in the fireplace in the lobby. A smiling lady, wearing a lanyard inscribed, volunteer, with the name "Barb" written below it, checked her in and directed her up the stairs to her room. She explained that the conference events would take place on the first floor.

The agenda Barb gave her looked promising. There was a welcome dinner, tonight, featuring a talk by the famous Northern Minnesota writer, Brent Brugger. All meals were provided and would be served in the resort's restaurant.

Starting tomorrow, there would be classes, workshops, and peer groups with plenty of time to also read, write, and get outside and try some winter sports, if so inclined. The opportunities to talk to an agent or editor came later in the week. Before that, Emma planned to attend a workshop on how to pitch your novel.

The second floor of the lodge looked like a typical small hotel. She found her room and opened the door, with an old-fashioned key that she had to jiggle, a bit, to get it to work. The room looked cute, with an old wooden dresser, and a double bed covered by a patchwork quilt, but it felt a little chilly and smelled a bit damp.

Maybe I'll spend more time downstairs, by the fire, she thought.

The evening meal was a buffet. While standing in line, the woman in front of her struck up a conversation by asking where she was from and what she was writing. After they sat down together, she introduced herself as Nan from Bemidji. Then, the man on the other side of Emma asked her much the same questions. Soon, they were all chatting, happily, through the meal. Emma realized that, since everyone was here on their own, and here for the same reasons, it would be easy to strike up a conversation.

She looked around the room at the several dozen other people attending. She was surprised to see Bryan, from her writers' group, sitting there wearing one of his trademark silk scarves. Why hadn't he mentioned that he was coming, too, when she told the group that she was going?

The keynote speaker, Brent Brugger, encouraged them to never give up on their dreams of becoming writers and talked about his writing journey. He said that he'd always wanted to write, but he was in his thirties when he got serious about it. At that time, he was still working a day job, so he'd formed the habit of getting up early, going to a coffee shop, and writing there for an hour before going to work. Now, when he no longer had to, he kept up the routine of getting up early to write. He said that he'd written for ten years before he sold anything, and that happened only after taking writing classes and changing genres. He'd always wanted to write the next great American novel, but he had found success writing mysteries.

Emma was surprised that he had struggled for so long. But she was encouraged by the thought that she had already changed genres. She had set aside her first attempt at a novel and started working on the family saga. Maybe she would be similarly fortunate. But she hoped it didn't take her ten years to get published.

Emma said goodbye to her new friends and caught up with Bryan.

"Hi, Bryan," she said. "I didn't expect to see you here."

"Oh, yeah. Hi, there. It was a last-minute decision. When you mentioned it, I investigated, and there was an opening. I guess not too many people want to come this far north the week before Christmas."

They arrived at the elevator, and Emma pressed the button. "I guess not. What did you think of the keynote speaker?"

"I've heard it all before."

"You've heard him speak, before?"

"Not him, specifically. But I've heard the "never give up your dream" speech. Although he did."

"He did what?" The elevator arrived, and they got in.

"He gave up his dream of writing the great American novel. Now, he just writes dreck."

"I don't know if that's fair. He's sold millions of books, and won awards."

Bryan said, primly. "If I can't write something important, I'd rather not write, at all."

The elevator stopped and they got out.

"Sure, I guess that makes sense. Well, see you later," Emma said.

That night, as she watched reruns on TV, she thought about her own writing goals. She wasn't as willing to give up, as Bryan seemed to be. She wanted to be a writer. So, she'd rather take the advice of a successful writer, like Mr. Brugger, and adapt to the market if need be. After all, now that he was famous, he was able to also write more serious literature. And, people were buying it, because they'd heard of him. Anyway, what was wrong with mysteries? She liked them.

After several days inside, with her head stuffed full of new ideas and information, Emma was ready for a change of pace. So, when her new friend, Nan, suggested trying cross-country skiing—something neither one of them knew how to do—Emma readily agreed.

They went to the equipment shed, where a cheerful teenager helped them select the right equipment, and showed them how to do it, then they went out on the groomed trail. Soon they were out of breath, and laughing at how hard it was. But Emma soon figured out the rhythm and was gliding along, until they came to a small hill.

"How is this supposed to work?" Emma said, as she tried to ski up the hill, and kept sliding back down, backward."

"I think we point our skis out. Look at those patterns in the snow," Nan said, pointing with her pole to the snow next to the track.

They stepped out of the tracks and gave it a try. Almost immediately, Emma stepped on one ski with the other one, and fell, laughing, into the loose powder. She struggled to her feet and tried it, again.

"I'm glad no one is out here to see how silly we look," Emma said.

Soon, they were swooping down the other side of the small hill at, what seemed like, a terrific speed. Emma fell, again, at the bottom of the hill.

After that, it was smooth sailing. Emma started to feel like she was getting the hang of it. Soon, they were back at the equipment shed, covered with snow, and sweating despite the cold, smiling, and laughing. They decided to go inside and have some hot cocoa.

After she got a mug of cocoa from the complimentary coffee bar, topped by as many mini marshmallows as she could fit into her cup, Emma sat down by the fireplace in the lobby with Nan. They compared notes on the conference and talked about their writing.

"I'm writing a memoir about taking care of my mother, in her final years," Nan said.

Emma looked at her, more closely. "You seem about my age, which is thirty. Aren't you too young to have had that experience?"

"Thanks, but I'm almost forty. My mom was in her forties when I was born, and she had early onset Alzheimer's."

"Are you married?" Emma asked.

"No, I never found Mr. Right."

"Oh, I'm sorry."

"I'm not. I've gotten used to being single, and I kind of like it. I come and go as I please. And, of course, I was able to be my mom's caretaker, without juggling my own family."

"How was that?"

"Hard, but rewarding. That's what my book is about. It's not depressing, at all. There are some sad moments, but there is also a lot of humor in it. I miss my mother."

"Have you finished your memoir?"

"Yes, except for a few finishing edits, I think it's done."

"And, do you think you'll go on writing?"

"I doubt it. This was something I needed to write as a transition, after spending years caring for my mom. Unless I have some other big experience in the future, of course."

Nan finished her cocoa and headed upstairs to change. Emma decided to sit by the fire, a while longer. She sat there, staring into the fire, contemplating the many different reasons people have for writing.

Chapter Seventeen

The rest of the week flew by. Emma joined a critique group with other historical novelists. Their comments were encouraging. She also took a workshop on how to write a query letter, and how to pitch your project.

Meanwhile, she watched with growing concern as the weather forecasts predicted a storm coming. Some people took off a day or two early, to beat the storm, but Emma didn't want to miss her chance to pitch her book. She had signed up for three 15-minute slots, with two agents and one editor. She was glad she had stayed, when the editor, and one agent, asked her to send them her first chapter.

Elated, she sat by the fireside in the lobby with a cup of coffee, basking in the moment, and planning how she would finish her book once she got home. So, she would be ready if, and when, she was asked to send the whole book. Bryan passed by and stopped.

"I wanted to talk to you about the billiards contest," he said.

"Oh? What about it?" Emma said. "By the way, thanks for coming. It was nice to see most of the Wordmasters there."

"No problem." He smoothed back his hair that had fallen over one eye. "Anyway, here's the thing." He hesitated.

Emma waited without speaking, puzzled by his manner.

He took a deep breath. "I was the one that hid the cue stick."

"You hid it? But, why?"

"Jessie put me up to it. When I passed her on my way to the men's room, she handed it to me and asked me to hide it behind the coat rack. She said it was a "joke." Haha." He made quotation marks around the word joke, with his fingers.

Emma thought about that for a moment. "Why did you go along with it? And, why didn't you say anything, when I started to look for it?"

"I was mad at you for getting on my case at the Wordmasters' meeting."

Emma tried to recall what she had said to him that he might have misinterpreted. Clearly, he was very thin-skinned.

"I'm sorry. I didn't mean to "get on your case," she said. "If I said anything that seemed... umm, unkind, I apologize."

"Apology accepted," he said, smugly. "And I'm sorry, too."

She looked at him with concealed amusement. "Forget about it. Not a problem."

After he left, Emma continued gazing into the fire. *He caught me at just the right time.* She chuckled to herself. *A week ago, I might have wanted to skin him alive. But I no longer care. Note to self, in the future, try not to say anything to Bryan that can be misinterpreted.*

THE NEXT MORNING, SHE awakened to the sound of howling winds. She went over to the window and looked outside at a white mass of swirling snow. She had planned to drive home this morning, but she couldn't drive in these conditions. And, even if the wind died down, her little hatchback wouldn't make it through snow drifts. She'd have to wait until the storm passed, and the roads were plowed. It didn't look like she'd be going home today.

Before she could contact her sister, telling her she planned to stay an extra day, her phone pinged with a text message from Lily. "Road conditions are bad. Better stay where you are. We'll take care of the kittens."

Emma texted back, "Okay."

When she went downstairs, she found that the crowd had thinned out. A few stragglers were helping themselves to the complimentary breakfast in the lobby. As usual, there was a fire burning in the fireplace. Emma took her yogurt, roll, and coffee and sat as close to the crackling fire as she could, and watched the swirling whiteness outside of the plate glass windows, while she ate. She felt a little lonely and abandoned. Tomorrow was Christmas Eve. She hoped she wouldn't have to spend it here, by herself.

With a sigh, she went back to her room. Then, she decided this would be a good time to write a scene where her characters coped with their first winter in Minnesota. She dove into her project, and the hours flew by.

Chapter Eighteen

The next day dawned clear and cold. Emma checked the traffic website. The roads were in good shape. She shouldn't have any trouble getting home, today. Then, she checked the temperature. Yikes! It was twenty below zero! Oh well, once the car warmed up, it wouldn't matter.

She had packed up most of her things before bed last night, so she just threw in a few last-minute items, and headed out. When she stepped outside, the cold was like a slap in the face.

That snow pile, over there, must be my car. I think that's where I parked, she thought.

She jogged across the nearly deserted parking lot, her suitcase bumping along behind her, over ridges of hardened snow left by the snowplow. When she got to her car, she swiped armloads of snow off the back of her car, opened the hatch, threw in her suitcase, purse, and backpack, and pulled out the long-handled snow brush, with an ice scraper on the other end of it.

After ten minutes of brushing snow, and scraping ice, she was covered with snow and shivering from the cold. Her fingers were freezing inside of her gloves, and her toes becoming lumps of ice, but at last, she could get into her car. She jumped in and turned the key. Then heard the depressing, click, click, click of a dead battery. She tried it again, hoping for a spark of life. Again, just click, click, click.

"Aargh, you stupid piece of tin!" She yelled as she pounded on the steering wheel.

Then, she got out and ran back inside to defrost. She spoke to the person at the registration desk and he sent the maintenance man out to jump her car. It still wouldn't start.

"Do you think I need a new battery," Emma asked.

"It could be that, or something else. I guess you'll have to call a garage. They might have to tow it in for repairs," he said.

They went back inside, and Emma made several calls to local garages. She found out that it would be hours before anyone could get there. And days before any repairs could be taken care of. Everyone was short-staffed, since it was Christmas Eve.

She texted Lily with the bad news.

A few minutes later, Lily texted back. "Help is on the way."

Emma hesitated; she didn't want to be a bother. She was sure that her brother-in-law had better things to do on Christmas Eve than rescue her. But she also didn't want to wait around here for hours. So, she just texted back, "Okay, I'm in the lobby."

Then she retrieved her backpack and purse from the car, called off the request for a tow from the local garage, and settled in to wait.

She looked up from scrolling through her phone, when she heard a vehicle pull up in front of the lodge. She saw a familiar truck, with chain-covered wheels. A burly figure, wearing a puffy, olive-drab parka, with a fur-lined hood, climbed out and headed inside. He blew in, followed by a blast of frigid air.

He threw back his hood, and Emma saw that it was Sam. She stood up and raised an arm in greeting, and he came over to her, while she started putting on her coat and gathering her things.

"Hi, Sam. Thanks for coming" she said.

"No problem. How's it going?" he asked.

"Not bad," she said, reflexively, then laughed. "Actually, it could be better. My car won't start."

"I know. That's why I'm here," he said.

"Sorry to drag you up here. I thought Lily would send Frank."

"Sorry to disappoint you."

"No, that's not what I meant." Emma felt flustered. "Just, that I didn't want to be a bother."

"No bother. Frank called me, and explained the situation. I volunteered, in case your car needs to be towed," he said. "Shall we?"

He headed toward the door. Emma grabbed her backpack and purse and followed him. He stopped at the door, waited for her to catch up, and held the door open for her.

"Meet you over at your car, and we'll see if we can get it started for you," he said, and then hopped into his truck.

Emma hurried across the parking lot and got into her car, shivering.

He drove over and parked, the front of his truck facing the front of her car, hooked up the battery cables, and they tried, several times, to get the car started.

"It won't start. And, it's not just a dead battery," he said.

They talked it over, and decided to tow the car home. Once underway, Emma glanced at Sam's profile, trying to judge his mood. He had seemed ticked off, the last time they talked.

"Have you had a busy morning?" she asked.

"Oh, yeah. Always, during these cold snaps." He smiled at her. "You're not the only one with a dead car."

He seems like his usual easygoing self. That's a good sign, she thought.

"How was your week?" he asked.

"Great. I learned a lot, and got a couple of requests for pages, from an agent and an editor." She recapped the week. "And, you'll never guess what I tried—cross-country skiing."

"No kidding? How'd it go?"

"Not too bad. I had a little trouble going uphill and fell a few times. But I think I got the hang of it. The lady I was with was a newbie, too. So, I didn't feel too dumb."

"Great," he said. "Maybe we could try it, together, sometime." He smiled at her, again.

Maybe he's over being mad at me, she thought. Emma wondered if she should bring up the billiards tournament, or just forget about it. She decided to try to clear the air.

"I had a weird conversation with Bryan," she said.

He glanced at her, sharply. "Who?"

"You know, from my writers' group. The guy from the Arts Center."

"Oh, yeah, Bryan, with a y." He rolled his eyes.

They both laughed.

"Anyway, he said that he was the one who hid the cue stick, during the tournament."

"What?"

Emma repeated their conversation.

"So, Jessie lied to me," Sam said.

"She did? You mean, you asked her about it?"

"Yeah. After I talked to you at church. Remember?"

"Oh, yes, I remember."

"I got to thinking, who had a better motive than Jessie? She's the type who would be mad about coming in third. So, I asked her, the next time I saw her. She swore, up and down, that she hadn't hidden it."

"Well, technically, that's true," Emma said. "She gave it to Bryan, and he hid it."

He snorted. "Same thing. They were in it, together. One thing, for sure, I am so done with her."

That assertion made Emma smile.

"Anyway, I just wanted to apologize for overreacting. I was out of line" she said. "The truth is, I should have gotten there on time, and tracked down my precious cue stick. Or, better yet, practiced more with some of the other sticks, so it wouldn't have been such a big deal."

"That's true. I just wish it hadn't happened, so I could have beaten you fair and square."

She looked at him in fake amazement. "Like you would have! *I* would have beaten *you*."

He laughed. "We'll never know, will we?" he said. "Unless—here's an idea—we have our own little contest, under ideal circumstances, and then we'll see who wins."

"As I recall, you still owe me a dinner from last time. Soon, you'll owe me another one."

They continued bantering, and laughing, all the way home, while Christmas carols played on the radio.

As they drove, Emma admired the scenery. The sky was crystal blue, with a few wispy white clouds. Glistening snow weighed down the branches of pine trees, and mounded in swirls and ridges in open spaces. It really was beautiful up here. It's true what they say, she reflected, there are places that resonate with you, where you feel most at home. This was her place.

As they pulled into her driveway, Emma said, "Thanks, again, for coming to my rescue. Do you have time to come in for a cup of coffee, or something?"

"Love to," he said. 'I'll be there in a minute." He went to detach her car from the tow bar.

Emma was taking out her key, when the door was flung open and she was greeted by Lily and the kids, and the odor of pine and coffee.

The two older kids were holding her kittens. There was a babble of voices as the kids all started talking, at once, saying something about a Christmas tree, and the kittens.

"You're home!" Lily exclaimed, hugging Emma. "Where's Sam?"

"Here I am," Sam said. He came up to the front door, carrying Emma's suitcase.

"I hope you don't mind," Lily said.

"Mind what?" Emma asked.

Lily led the way out of the crowded hallway, and into the living room, and gestured toward the Christmas tree in the corner. "This!"

Frank was removing some ornaments and putting them back into a cardboard box. "I'm taking off the breakable stuff, because of those little rascals." He pointed to the kittens. "Now, if they climb the tree, again, they won't break anything. Welcome home, Emma."

"I wasn't expecting this." Emma gazed at the tree, recognizing the ornaments her parents had used. "No, I don't mind, at all. It's beautiful."

"It was Sam's idea. He brought the tree and helped us put it up. Now, take off your things," Lily told Sam and Emma. "And then we'll all go into the kitchen. I made coffee and cocoa, and brought some Christmas cookies that I made."

After the coffee and cookies, Lily said the kids needed a nap, and she left with her family.

Sam and Emma refilled their coffee cups, took them into the living room, and sat on the couch, admiring the tree.

"You brought the tree," Emma said. "Why?"

"I heard about this deal, where you can get a permit to cut a tree from a national forest, as part of their forest management program. It sounded like fun, so I wanted to give it a try. I cut a couple of them, and gave one to Frank and Lily. I thought you might like one, too."

"Oh, I do. But what about your house?"

"I never put up a tree. That seems like a lot of trouble just for me."

They sat, silently staring at the tree for a few moments. The kittens crawled up on them and settled down for a nap, Midnight on Sam, and Tips on Emma.

"I suppose I should get going," Sam said. Without moving.

"I suppose so," Emma said. "Before you go, can I ask you something?"

"Of course."

"Are we dating?"

Sam laughed. "At last count, we have plans to play pool, go out to dinner, and go cross-country skiing. That sounds like dating, to me." He shifted sideways, and looked at her. "Is that okay with you?"

"Yeah, that's okay." Emma shifted sideways, in Sam's direction. It didn't seem to faze the kitten who just started purring. "Only..."

"Only what?" His gold-flecked eyes looked into hers.

She looked away. "I don't want to rush into anything. I rushed into my first marriage. I thought Harry was a sweet, sensitive guy. It turned out he was just lazy and controlling. If I fall in love, again, I want it to be forever."

Emma looked back at Sam, who was smiling at her.

"I want that, too. Can I tell you a secret?" he said.

"I think you better."

"I've had a crush on you since I was a kid, and you were a gawky girl. I saw you, one summer day, when I was about fourteen. You were coming out of the grocery store with an ice cream cone. I was sitting on a bench, outside of the store, drinking a can of pop. One look, and that was it. I was in love."

"Really?"

"Really. So, you see, there's no rush. I've already waited for almost twenty years; I can wait a while longer. Now, I really should be going. Other people to rescue, you know."

Sam detached the little black kitten from his lap, placed it on the couch next to him, then he leaned over and kissed her with a soft, tender kiss that sent ripples of pleasure throughout her body. When he stopped kissing her, she opened her eyes, breathless, and gazed into his beautiful eyes.

He broke the spell. "Sorry, I have to go. See you, tomorrow," he said, getting up.

"What's tomorrow?" she asked.

"Why, Christmas, of course," he said.

THE NEXT DAY, EMMA sat on one end of the pew next to Sam. Filling out the pew, little Tommy and Cindy fidgeted between Lily and Frank.

The children's choir was as cute as could be, as they sang Christmas carols after mass. The grade-school-aged kids were scrubbed, brushed, and in their Sunday best. It looked like they had been told to wear something Christmassy, and most of the kids pulled it off. Except one of the older boys, standing in the back, who wore a baggy grey t-shirt and jeans. Maybe he had forgotten, or he was rebelling, or maybe that was the best that he had.

Jenny, one of the youngest kids, was in the front row, wearing a white shirt under a red jumper. Her big smile showed off a missing front tooth, as they sang Silent Night. Emma grinned back at her, feeling absurdly happy. It seemed like they were, already, all one big family.

Chapter Nineteen

I t was early December, two years later. And Emma was sitting at a table in the gallery of the Arts Center, signing books. Her husband, Sam, sat at the front counter handling the book sales. Emma was finally celebrating her book launch. She had been amazed by how long the process had taken, from the first inklings of interest, almost two years ago, to the final product.

In the background, she heard Ray regaling a steady stream of townsfolk, who had drifted in to look at the exhibits on the history of Finish migration to Minnesota. He had created the exhibits, and he was in seventh heaven while sharing his vast storehouse of knowledge on the subject.

Bryan looked on, disapprovingly, and darted about picking up empty coffee cups and scowling at the muddy footprints left on the floor. He was a bit of a fuss budget, Emma thought, but it was nice of him to make the gallery available for her event.

When the townsfolk could break away from Ray's lecture, they stopped to congratulate Emma on her book release, and get their copies signed.

"How's it going?" Tania asked, holding out her copy for signing.

"Great!" Emma took the book from her. "I'm a little tired, right now." She placed a protective hand on her baby bump. "But I'm loving every minute of it."

"I guess you won't be entering the pool tournament this year," Tania said.

Emma signed the book and handed it back to Tania. "Nope. Neither of us will be. We're too busy getting the house ready for the baby."

Emma reflected that her house, rather, their house, was still under construction. It turned out that everything took longer than expected—both in home repairs, as well as in publishing. Luckily, the latest updates were confined to one upstairs bedroom that they were converting into a nursery. So, they could finally invite everyone to their house for Christmas, this year.

"Great. That gives the rest of us a chance," Tania said.

Emma laughed. "Sounds good."

She looked up to find Sam smiling at her, and she smiled back. I guess this is what "happily ever after" looks like, she thought.

Don't miss out!

Visit the website below and you can sign up to receive emails whenever Bonnie Oldre publishes a new book. There's no charge and no obligation.

https://books2read.com/r/B-A-XFBCB-IXASC

BOOKS 2 READ

Connecting independent readers to independent writers.

About the Author

Bonnie Oldre is a former librarian with a B.A. in English Literature from the University of Minnesota and an M.L.I.S. degree. She writes short stories, historical fiction, and historical mysteries. She lives in Minneapolis, Minnesota with her husband. Her novels include the mystery novels, *Silent Winter Solstice,* and *Flood of Memories*, set in late 1960s Northwestern Minnesota; and the WWII historical novel, *Caravans in the Dark.*

Read more at https://bonnieoldre.com.

9 798223 335412